A BLACKNESS ABSOLUTE

A COLLECTION OF SHORT HORROR

CAITLIN MARCEAU

"A sharp tongue stretching deep into the collective unconscious, like campfire stories, to divine a vast array of hells to chill you with. A Blackness Absolute stitches together Junji Ito-esque horrors that crawl into some atavistic part of your brain and take root there, shading your dreams with dread and uncertainty. Marceau has written a reflection on the terrifying ways in which time stains everything, unforgivably, into states of ruin. She cuts, with serrated edge, into the pure, disturbing imagination of nightmares, and sustains terror from start to finish. Creepy as hell. Utterly addictive and compellingly frightening. A remarkable ride I cannot recommend enough."

— Sofia Ajram, author of *Coup de Grâce*

Copyright © 2024 Caitlin Marceau
Cover Art © 2024 Ross Nischler
ISBN (ebook) 978-1-998851-87-4
ISBN (paperback) 978-1-998851-86-7
ISBN (hardcover) 978-1-998851-88-1

Magnum Opus was first published in 2022 by Timber Ghost Press
A Blackness Absolute was first published in 2023 by Ghost Orchid Press
Second edition published in 2024 by Hedone Books

To all my Halloween people.

CONTENTS

CONTENT WARNING

The stories that follow may contain graphic violence, gore, and themes
that may be upsetting to some readers.

Please go to the very back of the book for a detailed content warning
of each piece.

Beware of spoilers.

A BLACKNESS ABSOLUTE

The step groans underneath her weight. She grabs the rung of the ladder hard, her knuckles turning white as the wood digs into the fleshy part of her palm. Her heart is hammering so hard she swears she can feel the vibrations from it in her spine, and she wants to climb back out of the hole, but instead forces herself to go deeper inside. As she descends further into the earth, strong hands wrap around her waist and help lower her into the abandoned mineshaft.

"Not too bad, right?" Liam asks her.

"Right," she lies unconvincingly.

"According to the diagram my dad's friend gave me, we have one more ladder to go down at the end of this shaft and then we can *really* get exploring."

She feels the familiar tempo of panic thumping against her spine so she nods, keeping silent, wondering if her sudden migraine is from the panic of being underground, or from the headlamp squeezing her head tight. The light only illuminates the tunnel a few feet ahead of her, the darkness swallowing it up the further away the beam shines. Zoey follows her boyfriend towards the wall of black that threatens to devour them both, but never does. They walk through the narrow tunnel, dirt and rock crunching under their sturdy boots, the two-way radio clipped to her belt swinging back and forth, gently clanging against the plastic water bottle that hangs next to it, thumping into her leg with every step.

"How long did you say your dad worked here?" she eventually asks, when the silence becomes too much.

"Not for long. Maybe a year or two? The mine closed down shortly after he started working it, and then he and his crew were moved to the Kierens mine in Val-d'Or."

"That's quite the commute."

Liam laughs. "Yeah, well, he was happy to move closer to his family in Malartic. Hell, I think he was just happy to move closer to civilization. There's no one out here."

The thought chilled her.

Liam wasn't wrong, though. The mine was north of Villebois and had been abandoned since the early '80s, when the river of gold had seemingly run dry, and one of the smaller runoff tunnels had collapsed on a miner. The community that had sprung up around the mine had vanished just as suddenly as it had appeared. Now, all that was left were the kilometres of empty tunnels which ran under the ground and deep into the face of the mountain, and derelict houses that had never been sold, only abandoned when the local economy had collapsed. Although it wasn't much of a tourist spot, it brought the occasional adventurer, looking to explore the lush woods or the sprawling tunnels beneath the Earth's surface.

Unfortunately, Zoey was neither of these things. She hated the woods, with its insects and dangerous animals, and the idea of wandering a mine filled her with dread, not excitement. But when Liam's dad had passed away of lung cancer earlier that spring, he'd felt compelled to adventure to the places that had marked his father's youth, in an attempt to reconcile the loss and reconnect with the man who'd raised him. So, secretly reluctant, she had joined him on the nearly nine-hour drive from Montreal to the middle of nowhere so he could finally visit the mine his father had once worked in during a sliver of his youth. Zoey hoped the trip was cathartic for him, because she had no plans of making it again.

He stops at the lip of another opening, bending down to inspect the wood of the ladder. It must seem sturdy enough because he begins to make his way down, moving slowly as he tests his weight on each rung before stepping onto it freely. Zoey follows, jaw clenched, as the space gets even darker. The videos hadn't been lying when they said there was no light inside a mine, and while she had been expecting it to be dark, she hadn't expected it to be so absolute.

Liam digs the map out of the pocket of his bag and lays it on the ground, his headlamp illuminating the worn paper. He traces his finger along one of the blue tunnels, the lines and notes meaning little to Zoey. He smiles up at her while he folds the paper and puts it back in his pocket.

"Okay, so as long as we stick to this tunnel and don't veer off down any of those little side tunnels, we should be okay and have an easy enough time navigating everything. And as long as we're within a clear line of each other, we shouldn't have any trouble with the radios."

He unclips his radio from his belt and turns the knob at the top. There's a soft click as the two-way comes to life, and he presses the button on its side as he speaks into the receiver. "Can you hear me?"

Her radio is silent. She takes it off her belt and turns it on while he tries again.

"Can you hear me?" he asks, his voice now ringing clearly from her device.

"Yes," she says into her radio, her voice sounding clear from the two-way in his hand.

He clips the radio back onto his belt and smiles at her. "Good! Okay, let's get exploring!"

He takes off down the shaft, and although Zoey knows he expects her to take off in the opposite direction, she follows him down his length of the tunnel. The air is thick and makes her chest hurt, and she desperately wants to turn back around and climb out of the hole she followed him into, but she knows how important the trip is to Liam. So she stays.

"Can you believe my dad used to be in this tunnel, all day, six days a week, from sunup to sundown?"

Zoey remembers his pale, sickly form in the hospice bed, fingers stained black from years underground, his lungs riddled with disease thanks to decades spent in bad air, breathing dangerous gases. She can.

"It must have been difficult for him, not getting to see the sun like most people do, always spending his time in the dark. I wonder why he did it for so long."

"He loved it. The man was practically a mole. I think the hardest part for him was being forced to give it up. He wasn't the same when he lost his job. It's like he didn't know who he was anymore. I think he'd have kept mining until the day he—OW!"

Liam stops dead in his tracks, hissing under his breath.

"What's wrong?"

"I think I stepped on a fucking nail."

He stands on one foot and tries to turn the other towards him, grabbing his ankle to hold the leg steady, but loses his balance and lands hard on the sore foot. Liam cusses loudly, hissing between clenched teeth as he limps to the side of the tunnel and leans against one of the wooden support beams to look at his injury, dirt and a few pebbles coming loose from above.

CRACK!

The noise is deafening, and the two of them look at each other in confusion. Zoey's heart nearly stops as she watches the support beam behind Liam shift, the rotted wood finally giving way after doing its job for forty-plus years. What starts off as a light shower of dirt is quickly an avalanche of earth and stone. Zoey screams, turning on her heel and trying to run from the onslaught of ground raining down on them. The headlamp is no match for the cascade of land, as it falls heavily around her and blackens out all light in the cramped space. She moves as fast as her legs will carry her, but it's not fast enough. The wind is knocked out of her as rocks pummel her body and heavy earth buries her deep beneath it, the shaft bathed in noise so loud it feels like thunder.

And just as suddenly as it began, the tunnel is silent.

Zoey coughs, expelling dirt from her lungs. The bitter taste of it coats the inside of her mouth and makes her eyes sting. Her chest hurts, lungs tight, and she moves her hand through pebbles and rock shards. Her skin is bruised and cut, and it's only as she's pulling herself free of the heap does she realize she's crying hysterically. The head-lamp is thankfully unbroken, and while the tunnel has caved in behind her, it's still mostly intact up ahead. Although the ceiling of the tunnel seems to have sagged a good four feet—crawling room only—there's still a hope of escape.

Her panic quickly gives in to relief, which turns to panic once more when she realizes Liam, and the exit, are behind her.

"Liam?" she calls, voice muffled and throat sore. She unclips the water bottle from her belt and lets out a small sob when she realizes it's been cracked. The water is mostly drained from the bottle, trails of wet sprawling over the stone around her, but there's just enough for her to rinse her mouth of the dust. "Liam!" she screams louder now.

Silence.

She sits on the ground and breathes slowly, trying to prevent the rising hysterics. The air is thick and heavy, and she can taste it even with her mouth closed. The rock dust coats the inside of her nose and the back of her throat, and covers her skin and hair in a sheet of grey. She takes stock of her injuries and is relieved to see that, apart from a few scratches and bumps, she's largely unhurt. Something crackles by her side in the dirt, and it takes her a moment to realize that her two-way radio has come free of her belt. She digs through the rocks and finds the small plastic device.

"... there? Zoey? Are ... there?"

Relief washes over her as she holds the radio close to her mouth, pressing the button on its side. "Yes! Liam! Are you okay? Can you hear me?"

"Zo- ... can't ... you. Where ... you?"

"I'm on the other side of the cave-in!" "Where?"

"On the other side of the cave-in!"

"Okay ... to me ... the map says to ... follow the ... then right! Not ... to the end of the hall, then ... right. Okay?"

"You're cutting out. I can't hear you!"

"Follow the path ... the end. Then ... need to turn right ... Go to the end ... make another right!"

"So I go to the end of the tunnel, turn right, go to the end, and turn right again?"

"Yes! The map ... it should ... get to me."

The thought of moving through the blackness alone sends her into a cold sweat, but she knows the exit, and Liam, are on the other side of the rock wall. If she's going to get out, the only way there is through the mine.

"Okay! I'm coming to you. Don't move!"

"... careful!"

She clips the radio back onto her belt and begins to crawl through the rubble, the sharp stones digging into her arms and legs as she maneuvers through the tunnel, ripping into her jeans and cutting through her thick sweater. Before long, she knows she's bleeding. The minutes feel like hours in the void under the Earth. The only thing that reminds her of the passage of time is her lungs, burning in her chest, and the dryness in her mouth. She keeps licking her lips, trying to keep them from splitting in the dirty air, but it only makes them worse.

Finally, she begins to reach the end of the tunnel, the ceiling getting taller, and giving her a chance to stand back up. She brushes herself off, wincing as her hands skim over the raw skin on her knees, the blue denim soaked with her blood appearing brown in the dim light. She takes the radio from her belt and presses the button, speaking into it excitedly.

"I'm at the fork. I'm going right," she tells him.

He doesn't answer.

"Liam, can you hear me?"

Silence.

Sweat beads along her forehead and rolls down her back as she looks down the tunnel into the nothingness that waits for her. She turns the two-way radio off and on before trying to contact Liam again, but the line stays dead. She knows why they're not working—*as long as we're within a clear line of each other, we shouldn't have any trouble with the radios*—but it doesn't bring her any comfort as she looks into the darkness of the abandoned mine. She doesn't want to go forward, she wants to go back, but she can't.

She slowly makes her way through the new tunnel, stumbling over the uneven ground. It seems that unlike the main passage, the runoff tunnels were either made hastily or more severely impacted by the passage of time. The ground is littered with jagged stones and large rocks, and dust makes the air thick like seafoam. Zoey feels like she's breathing through a burlap sack, and her chest is tired from the effort of it. She moves further into the tunnel, wondering how far she is from the end, when her headlight goes out.

She freezes in her tracks and fumbles with the light, turning it off and then back on. It's weak and flickers. She knows it's only a matter of time before it goes off completely and she's alone in the dark. Her eyes burn and her legs want to buckle, but she tries to breathe slow and think rationally. She walks across the narrow tunnel until the tip of her right hand is brushing against the tunnel wall. She needs to turn right, which she should be able to feel in the stone. She turns the headlamp off and keeps moving along the dark hall, breathing slow and steady. When she feels the wall turn inwards, she turns the light on to make sure it's the final turn, but it's a side-channel turning off of the main one. She keeps going straight and shuts the light off again, the sound of her breathing echoing around her.

As she moves through the mine shaft, she slowly begins to make out specks of silver and gold shimmering along the wall. She realizes with a start it's because there's a soft light at the end of the tunnel. A man stands at the end of the tunnel, his headlight stretching out ahead of him.

"Liam!" she practically sobs, feet moving even faster along the rocks.

He turns and makes his way down the tunnel, moving nimbly over the stone and uneven pathway. She's tempted to shout for him to slow down, but she's as desperate as he is to leave the mine. As he gets to the end of the tunnel, he makes a left turn and continues down a narrow path into the darkness.

"I thought you said we had to go right?" she calls, voice too loud in the confined space. If he answers her, she doesn't hear it from how far away he is. She stands at the fork in the path and is about to argue when the light begins to fade from around her. Not wanting to be left alone in the dark, she follows after him.

This tunnel is narrower than the last, and as she moves through the mountain she can feel the passage growing narrower and narrower. Her lungs are struggling to draw in oxygen and she's tired enough that she doesn't have the energy to call out for Liam to wait. She just crawls behind him through the rock, her arms and legs burning with each inch forward. A wooden beam lies across their path, but Liam is able to lift part of it up and get himself past it. As Zoey approaches, she realizes the space is too small to fit her and the beam too heavy for her to lift.

"Liam! Wait!"

He doesn't answer.

She tries to squeeze herself under the beam, but the radio on her belt stops her. She unclips it and holds it in her right hand and tries again. She gets both arms through, then her head, then her chest, then she sucks her stomach in as far as it will go as she pulls herself with her arms under the beam, propelling herself forward with her legs. The pressure on her chest is almost unbearable, but she keeps pushing forward anyway, trying to get beneath the beam to freedom. She gets about halfway into the space but can't fit her hips past the beam.

Panic rises in the back of her throat, and she pushes herself backwards with her hands, trying to move back into the main tunnel, but she doesn't budge. It's hard to breathe as she's sandwiched between the rock and the beam, and she thrashes in terror as she realizes she's stuck.

"Liam! Help me!" she wheezes into the darkness, all traces of Liam —and his light—gone. She squeezes the button on her two-way radio. "Come back, please!"

"What?" Liam says, voice choppy and static-laden.

"I need you to come back! I'm stuck," Zoey whispers, dizzy from the effort and lack of air.

"I haven't left ... tunnel. What ... you talking about?"

"You were here! You were with me!"

"No ... not. I'm stuck ... the beam ... on my leg. I can't move ... can't breathe. Please ... help... need help."

She drops the radio and turns on her headlamp, vision blurring at the edges as her pulse hammers in her ears, her lungs on fire as they struggle to get oxygen. The tunnel ahead of her is caved-in and impossible to navigate, the air thick with dust and rot. A wall of stone blocks the way forward, a crushed headlamp at its base.

"Help ... Zoey ... please. I can't ... move. Where ... you?" Liam's voice calls through the radio, voice sounding far away.

The light flickers once more before going out, the blackness around her absolute.

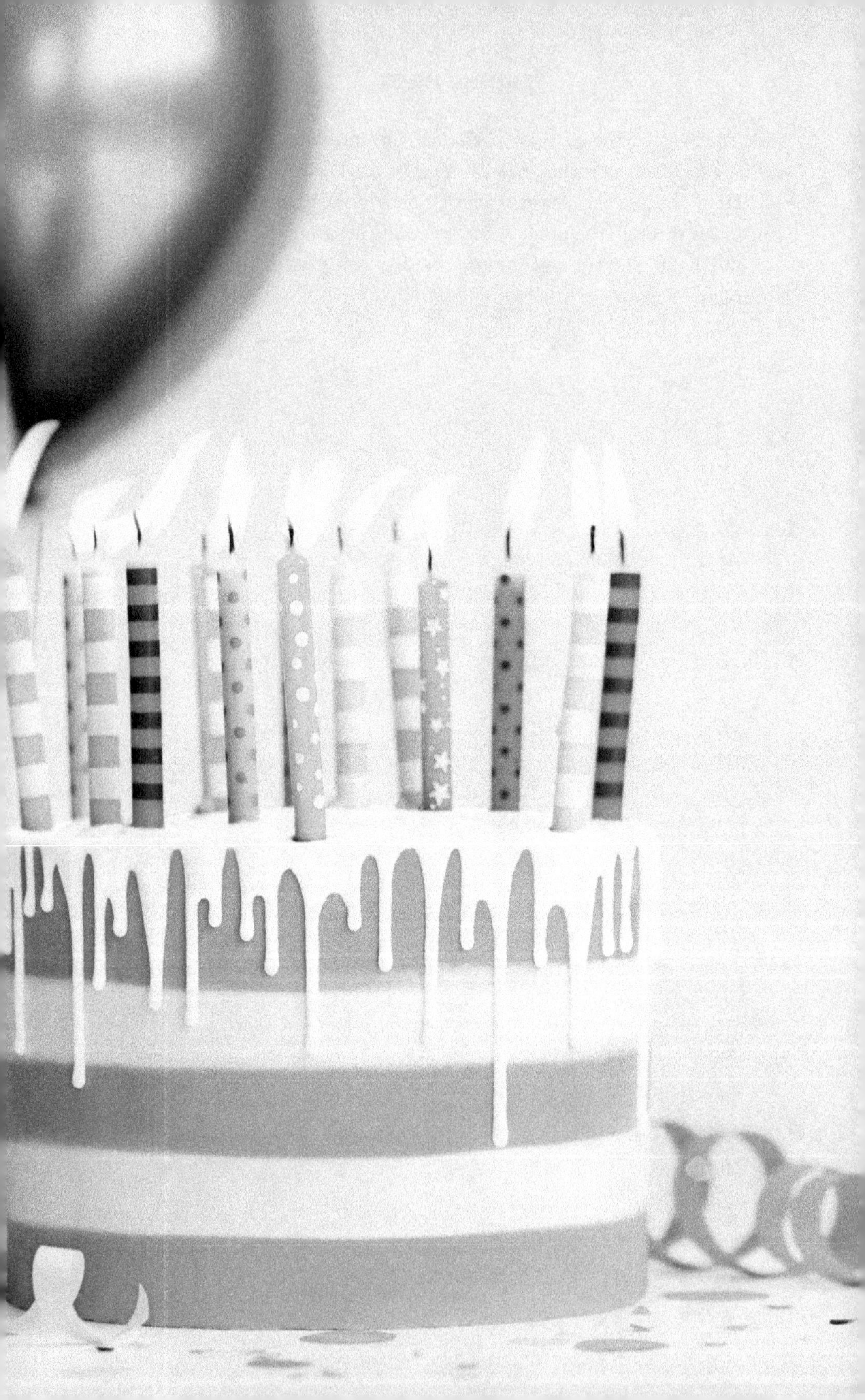

SARAH

She runs a tongue over her tooth, the bitter berry lipstick quickly disappearing from her pearly smile. She squints at her reflection, her features blending together in the dimly lit room, and imagines herself as one of the Hollywood actresses she sees on the giant posters outside the cinema, and which her mom's always reading about in the tabloids. She arranges her hair around her face, mentally trading her mousy brown locks for strands rich like dark chocolate, and trying to picture herself as Audrey Hepburn. Sarah's so lost in her own fantasy that she doesn't hear the front door slam shut. It's only when she hears his gruff voice and footsteps ascending the stairs that she realizes her father's home.

She licks her lips thick with spit and uses the sleeve of her shirt to try and wipe the colour off as he opens the door.

"Sarah, sweetie, your mother says it's time for—what the hell are you wearing?"

"Nothing!"

"You look like a damned harlot!" he shouts, bursting into her room. He snatches the tube off her vanity and grabs her roughly by the wrist, pulling her out of her bedroom behind him.

"Muriel, did you know about this?"

"About what?" her mom calls up from the kitchen.

"About our daughter making herself up like a slut!"

"Dad!"

"It's just a bit of rouge, Clifford," she says, poking her head into the stairwell and looking up at them. "It's hardly the end of the wor—"

"And if someone from the parish sees? How do you think my congregation's going to react if they found out my daughter—*my daughter*—was walking around town painted up like a damned Jezebel?" he screams, saliva spattering Sarah's face, his skin burning red with rage. "Take that filth off your face and get ready for supper."

He jerks her arm in the direction of the bathroom, catching her off guard. She clumsily falls to the floor, grateful not for the first time that her house has carpeting, before hurrying down the hall to the washroom. She closes the door, locking it behind her, and runs the water loudly as she tries to catch her breath. She grabs a washcloth off the nearby shelf and wets it with hot water before scrubbing her mouth, trying to avoid staring at her reflection in the harsh fluorescent light of the bathroom. She scrubs for a while, streaks of deep pink staining the white cloth. When the cotton finally comes away clean, she reluctantly looks at herself in the mirror.

Her bottom lip is red from the friction, as are the sides of her upper lip. It's the central divot between them, just under her right nostril, that's still streaked with berry. She wets the cloth and scrubs at the makeup, making sure to maneuver it in the tight crevice of her upper lip.

It's been there her whole life, and yet, somehow, it's only in these past few months that her cleft lip has been the main source of her anxiety. Being homeschooled through her primary years had kept her safe from (most of) the cruel things children say about those who don't fit in, and being the daughter of the town's Lutheran pastor only ever brought her kind words on Sundays. But since late August, when her parents felt a more public education would do her good, she's been plagued with anguish over the split in her lip and the mean things her peers whisper when they think she can't hear them or when they secretly hope she does.

Once the last of the lipstick has been scrubbed clean, she splashes cold water on her face, washes her hands, and dries them off with a towel before reluctantly unlocking and opening the door. She pokes her head out into the hall and checks to see if her father's waiting for her, not wanting to try his patience. But seeing that the coast is clear, she rushes to her room, changes into a different shirt—she doesn't want to think about how mad he'll be if he sees the smears of colour on the blouse of her uniform—and makes her way downstairs.

Her father is already seated at the head of the dinner table with a serving of ham, mashed potatoes, and peas heaped onto his plate. He grabs the cloth napkin from his table setting and tucks it into the collar of his dress shirt and waits for the rest of the family to join him, forearms resting on the table. Her mother hurries into the dining room from the kitchen, carrying two plates. She sets them down, one at the opposite end of the table and the other in the middle, before heading back into the kitchen. This time when she comes out, she's carefully carrying two glasses of water and a very full glass of sparkling wine. She places them carefully on the table, making sure to put the wine down first, before taking a seat across from Clifford. The two of them wait for him to say grace and take his first bite before they start eating.

"So," he says with a smile that never quite reaches his eyes, "how was your day, honey?"

"It was fine. Did some laundry and I finally cleaned the den, like I wanted to."

It's the standard answer she gives every night; she cleaned something and then tidied something else up.

"Did you? The den doesn't look vacuumed."

"I didn't get around to it. I was too busy dusting."

"Then make sure to do that tomorrow. Cleanliness is next to godliness, and I don't like dusty carpets," he tells her, taking another bite of the honey-glazed ham.

"Of course, dear," she says, running on auto-pilot.

He points to the table with his knife. "Where's the mustard?"

"It's in the fridge."

"I'd like some."

When Muriel takes another bite of her food and makes no move to get up, he slams his hand down. The table shakes from the force of it, water sloshing onto the tablecloth. The wine rocks back and forth in the glass, but thankfully she's had enough that it doesn't spill. She picks the stemware up and walks to the kitchen.

"And how was your day?" he asks Sarah, back to smiles again.

"It was okay."

"What did you learn at school today?"

"Nothing much."

"If you're not learning, you're not working hard enough. I'm sure you were taught a lot more than 'nothing' today, right?"

"Yes, sir."

"So then what did you learn?"

Sarah opens her mouth to answer but is grateful for her mother's timing. She carries another full glass of wine in one hand, a small bowl of mustard in the other, and puts them down on the table indelicately.

"And how was your day, *dear?*" she asks, drinking deeply from her cup.

"It was good. I had a call with the Lakeside Heights minister, Charles, for the upcoming joint fundraiser for the Children's Hospital. Which, by the way, you're going to need to cook three-dozen cupcakes for, some muffins, a few bundt cakes, and something else. I don't care what, just make it taste good and fresh. And make sure to dress up when the time comes. I won't have you covered in flour, looking like a small-town rube. I've already marked it on the calendar so you won't forget."

She nods, stabbing sharply at a small pile of potatoes on the centre of her plate. He doesn't notice her silence, or the far-away look in her eyes, and keeps talking.

"Then I went over to the Beauchamps place because they were having marital issues. His wife doubted his authority—lemme tell you, she's got some lip on her—so we went over some scripture together. We talked about her doubts, about Adam's divinely given right over Eve, and I left them with a few passages and worksheets to contemplate and complete for next week. Hopefully, it restores his faith in his marriage and helps get her back in line. The poor man." He laughs to himself at some unsaid joke and shovels more food in his mouth.

A few moments pass in silence, both of her parents lost in thought, before Sarah finally speaks.

"May I have a party at the house on Friday night?"

"I beg your pardon?" he asks, wiping his mouth with the serviette.

"For my birthday, I was hoping it would be alright to have a party."

"We were going to go to the steakhouse with your grandparents on Friday for your birthday. Did you not want to do that?"

"No, I did. I do! It's just, Friday is the only time I thought would work. I know that Sunday is your day, you know?"

"Sunday is God's day, Sarah."

"Yes, of course. I just meant that I know you get up really early in service of Jesus' message on Sunday, so you go to sleep early the night before. I know that Saturday is when you finalize your sermon and the lesson plan for Sunday school, so I wouldn't want to distract you with a party that day. But I thought, I don't know, maybe we could do supper on Saturday, and I could have a small party on Friday night. Maybe invite a few friends from school or something."

He crumples the cloth napkin in his hand.

"The same friends who told you to doll yourself up like a slut?"

"No, Dad! I swear, they didn't tell me to do anything."

"So then you decided you wanted to parade yourself around like a piece of meat on your own? If that's the case, you don't deserve to have a birthday at all."

"Dad, plea—"

"Shameful of you. I thought I raised you better than that."

"I was just trying to fit in," she says quietly, staring down at her plate. "If I just had the operation for my birthday. If you just let them fix my li—"

Clifford throws his balled-up napkin on the ground and slams his hands down on the freshly waxed surface hard, nearly knocking over the unused mustard, and shoving his chair back from the table.

"For fuck's sake!" he screams, voice loud enough that Sarah flinches. "Not this again! It was God's will for you to look this way! And defying the will of our Lord is more of an abomination than you will ever be. Are you telling me that you know more than God?"

"No! No, of course not, I just—"

"That you're privy to His divine plan?"

"I don't want the kids at school to make fun of me anymore, so my friends said they're trying to help make me pretty."

"Oh, so your wants are more important than what God has ordained. Is that it?" When she doesn't answer, he slams his fists onto the table for effect. "I asked you a question!"

"No, my wants aren't more important than the plan of our Lord."

"You're damned right they're not! He gave you the gift of life, and this is how you pay Him thanks? By exercising your vanity and ungratefulness? You should be humbled He chose to give you loving parents in the service of His word. And now you're trying to spit in the face of what He's created." He shakes his head. "And then you have the gall to ask if you can invite those whores over, to *my* house no less, for a party."

"I'm sorry. I shouldn't have asked. I didn't mean to offend you, Dad," she says, unable to look him in the eyes.

"They're bad influences, those loose girls. They don't really like you. You know that, right? They're just trying to corrupt you. Lead you to sin. I don't like them, not one bit." He chugs the last of his water and gets up from the table. He makes his way into the den, humming to himself.

"You can have your party on Friday, sweetie," her mother lazily tells her from the other end of the table. Her glass is empty, and her cheeks flushed. "I'll talk to your father, don't you worry about that. But Sarah, if those girls are trying to make you look another way, if they're trying to get you to be like them because they don't like how you already are, then they're not your real friends. And I hate to say it, but your father might have a point about them."

"They're just trying to be nice, Mom."

"They're trying to be mean, and dressing their cruelty up as 'good intentions.' But nothing your father or I can say will convince you of that. It's a lesson you need to learn on your own when you're good and ready."

She stands from her seat and begins gathering up the dishes. She kisses the top of Sarah's head as she picks up Clifford's dishes, frowning at the untouched mustard but keeping her thoughts to herself.

"Come on, help me bring everything to the kitchen."

Sarah does as she's told, collecting her dishes along with the salt and pepper shakers. She places the dirty china in the sink and the seasoning on the butcher's block. Her mother grabs a pill bottle off the counter, swallowing two Lorazepams with the remainder of the sparkling wine in the bottle before filling the sink with hot, soapy water.

"Now, go finish your homework. I have a headache, and I'm going to lie down for a bit. And the next time you're inspired to try on my lipstick, make sure your father is working late."

She nods, embarrassed, before heading off to her room.

———

THE BELL RINGS, and Sarah rushes down the stairs, barely avoiding a collision with her father as he goes to open the door.

"Be careful!" he shouts. "Answer the door like a lady, not a dog."

"Sorry, Dad."

"I have half a mind not to answer," he hisses viciously, "but your mother already spent my damned money on this party."

Sarah mumbles an apology but doesn't say much else for fear of making anything worse. She prays none of her friends will decide to get bold and ring the bell a second time; her dad wouldn't like that one bit.

After keeping her in suspended anxiety, he unlocks the heavy door and throws it open with a smile.

"Well hello, hello!" he says pleasantly to the group of young women on his stoop. "Now who do we have here?"

The girls introduce themselves—Deborah, Minnie, Audrey, Beatrice, and two other names he won't bother to remember—and disingenuously praise Clifford for his weekly sermons.

"My mom always looks forward to your sermons," Audrey politely lies. The other girls nod their heads in agreement, as if they can somehow confirm her mother's excitement.

"That's very kind," he says with a smile. "Now, Sarah will show you to the basement where the party is. Unfortunately, her mother is resting with a headache, and I don't want the noise to disturb her," he continues. He leaves out the part about how Muriel has had a headache since the day they got married, and how she's been popping pills since her sedatives became available for prescription.

"Yes, sir, Pastor McCullough," the girls say in near unison.

Sarah leads them through her house, bringing them to the basement door.

"Sarah, would you mind if I speak to you a moment?" She nods in agreement and steps to the side. "You girls go on down for now, she'll be along soon."

They run down the stairs, whispering and giggling among themselves, while the birthday girl waits behind. Her father turns to her, all traces of good humour gone from his face.

"So help me, Sarah, if they spill any pop on the carpet, or get crumbs all over the couch, it'll be you who pays to replace or clean them. You hear?"

"Yes, Dad."

"And if you finish the party snacks, that's too bad. It's all you're getting until I barbecue the burgers later. I won't have your gaggle of slutty girls eating me out of house and home. Am I clear?"

"Crystal clear, dad. I promise we'll all behave."

"Those girls are trouble, and I don't trust a damn word that comes out of their mouths. If you're hanging out with them, then I'll take everything you say with a grain of salt, too."

He hands her a bowl of chips and a platter stacked with tomato pizza cut into squares. She descends the steps carefully, making sure not to spill anything onto the new beige carpet her father is so concerned about.

Downstairs, her friends have gathered around the folding table her father erected at the back of the room, just under the window overlooking the grass of the backyard. A cheap plastic tablecloth with balloons printed on it is draped across the table. Crowding the surface are bottles of pop, a spot for the punch bowl that's still in the fridge, some cups, a chef 's knife on a pile of paper plates, and a stack of napkins. Audrey is pouring all the girls a glass of knockoff Coca-Cola, laughing to them about something. When one of them sees Sarah, the room gets quieter.

She brings the snacks to the table as the girls move away, each taking a seat on the furniture around the room. Sarah pours herself a glass of cream soda and, realizing all the chairs have been taken, grabs herself a spot on the ground.

"So," Audrey says, "got anything good to listen to, like Elvis?"

"Oh, um, my dad won't let that kind of music in the house. But I think I have the newest Patsy Cline album, if you want?"

"Ew," Minnie laughs. "You like Patsy Cline?"

"She's okay, I guess."

"The Beach Boys and The Beatles are good," Minnie insists.

"The Crystals are cool," Beatrice adds from across the room. "Patsy Cline is so boring."

"Ha, yeah, she is," Sarah agrees.

"I thought you liked her?" Audrey says, crossing her arms over her chest.

"Oh, uh, no. I mean, *I* don't like her. My mom does. I mean, she's not the worst or anything, but no way do I want to listen to her."

"So then why did you suggest her record?"

"I don't know. I just, I guess it was the first thing I could think of that wasn't gospel. But we have gospel music, if you'd like?"

Audrey smiles, but it's void of sincerity. "No, thanks. Go get your makeup, we'll do makeovers."

"I don't have any."

"What?"

Sarah looks down at her tunic dress. She fumbles with the cuff on one of her knee-high socks before the weight of their stares gets too heavy, and she reluctantly answers them.

"I don't have any makeup. My dad doesn't let me wear it. He says I'm too young, and that it's indecent for women to be vain."

"Your dad sounds like a lot of fun," Deborah says. The other girls laugh.

Audrey gets up from the couch and crosses the room to where her purse rests on the floor. She opens it up and pulls out a stick of light pink lip gloss, a compact, blush, some eyeliner, and a tube of mascara.

"Well, at least I never leave the house unprepared. Get over here, I'll make you pretty for your birthday."

The girls snicker, and Sarah's heart drops. She wants desperately to say yes, but knows her father will be enraged if she does. She's already tested his patience by having her friends over, and she knows more than a scolding will be in store for her after they leave if he finds her with makeup on.

"I can't. My dad won't let me."

Audrey frowns. "That's unfortunate. Well, guess it's your turn, Minnie!"

The girls laugh and maneuver themselves into a small circle on the floor. Sarah gets a slice of pizza and watches them from the other side of the room.

———

SHE HOLDS OPEN the green garbage bag as the group throws their paper plates and unfinished hamburgers away. She's still hungry, but seeing how little the rest of the girls were eating made her not want to finish the food her father grilled up, and she can't help but feel a little remorseful over the uneaten portion of her mother's potato salad that she threw away (especially since she asked her mother to make it special for her).

"So, ready for gifts?" Audrey asks. Sarah lights up at the suggestion.

"You guys brought me gifts?"

"It's a birthday party, of course we did. Well, it's actually just one gift, but we all pitched in for it."

She hands Sarah a thick envelope. It's decorated with stickers of birthday cakes and bright blue party hats. The girls gather together and watch as Sarah opens the gift excitedly. She pulls out a generic birthday card, a pile of gifts painted in watercolours on the front, and the standard "Happy Birthday!" printed inside. Less standard is the pile of cash tucked inside the card, and the address scrawled in blue cursive below the birthday well-wishes.

Doctor Henry Fisher
11150 Mountain Drive, Unit C.
Edmonton, Alberta, T5R 3K7

"What is all this?" Sarah asks, card in one hand and almost $150 in the other.

"It's your gift from all of us... and a few of the other kids at school. We didn't know what to get you, so we settled on getting you a new mouth."

"What?"

"Your lip," Audrey says, pointing at Sarah. "It's disgusting. Do you know how hard it was to eat while having to look at that thing? No way."

"It's freaky," Minnie quips beside her, "and everyone thinks so."

"So we thought we'd pay for you to have it fixed. Or, you know, at least put some money towards it. That way we don't have to look at it."

"It's gross," Deborah says matter-of-factly.

"And, honestly, this way our parents won't force us to hang out with you," Audrey finished.

"What ... what do you mean?" Sarah wants to cry but doesn't. Years of dealing with her father have taught her that crying only makes every- thing worse, and thankfully she's learned how to keep her tears at bay.

"You're weird. Your whole family's weird. Everyone thinks so, but nobody says anything because your dad's our minister and we'd get in trouble for excluding the church freak. At least if you get that *thing* fixed, you can make your own friends. Maybe even fit in with the rest of the Bible thumpers at school. And if that money's not enough," she tells Sarah, passing her a second gift, "then at least you'll have this to hold you over in the meantime."

Sarah drops the money and card onto the ground next to her and takes the small bag from Audrey. In it is a Halloween mask with makeup applied to the cheap plastic shell. The girls laugh at their clev- erness as Sarah stares at the mask.

"Happy birthday," Audrey calls out as Sarah walks slowly away from the girls, feeling sick, and slowly heads back upstairs. "Don't forget to bring down the cake!"

———

CLIFFORD STARES at the open book on his desk. His eyes hurt from looking at the numbers and praying for them to change. He does this every year around her birthday, and every year yields the same result: not enough money to fix her damned lip.

He always considered himself a good man. Doing the Lord's work, living a modest life, trying to be a good pastor. And then, when they had trouble conceiving, he thought the Lord was testing his faith, and so he prayed hard until he was blessed with a child. When she was born deformed, he saw it as an opportunity for spiritual growth. When Medicare wouldn't cover the operation because it was a cosmetic, not corrective, procedure, he saw His will in this too; a chance for him to prove himself a man through the sweat of his brow. Through hard work, faith, and by serving his flock, the Lord would provide.

But He didn't.

With each passing year the price for her surgery has only risen, while money gets tighter and tighter. Her face serves as a reminder of his failures as a provider, a mockery of his now-wavering faith, and the daughter he once considered a gift from God seems to have been sent from hell itself.

Tired and defeated, Clifford shuts the book and opens the door to his study, stretching in the hallway before making his way to the kitchen. His stomach grumbles, and he opens the refrigerator door, eager to tear into the night's leftovers. He moves Sarah's cake out of the fridge and onto the butcher's block before taking out the plate of hamburgers. As he takes out the ketchup, it dawns on him that while she's remembered to bring the punch downstairs, her cake is still untouched.

"Stupid bitch," he cusses to himself. "Sarah," he shouts, "your cake is still here!" He stands by the door, waiting for her to get the food. When the basement remains suspiciously quiet, he opens the door in annoyance. "I said come get your cake!"

She doesn't answer.

He swears under his breath and picks up the cake, ready to throw it down the stairs at her, but stops when he sees the empty bottle of Lorazepams at the bottom of the steps.

"Sarah?"

Silence. He puts the cake down on the table before heading into the basement.

The room is uncomfortably quiet. Sarah sits in the centre of the room, her back to her father. The girls lie in a circle around her. At first, he thinks they're playing a strange and lazy game, but then he notices the scarlet stains on the carpet—the carpet! How many times had he told that clumsy bitch to be careful?

"Sarah, what the fuck is going on?"

The punch bowl on the table is half empty. The bottom of the decorative glass is coated in a white powder, thick and undissolved.

As he draws closer, he realizes she's cradling her friend's head in her lap. The girl is asleep, or maybe unconscious, he can't tell, and only when he maneuvers around Sarah does he realize what his daughter's done.

She points to Audrey with the chef's knife. Like the other girls, her top lip has been sliced off, her pink gums and white teeth exposed.

"You know, Dad," Sarah says, looking at him with the same dead-eyed smile he's worn before, "I don't think I need that operation after all."

THE BROOMWAY

The mud is thick and heavy, and it coats the bottom of his worn leather boots, making the trip back harder than it has to be. It's his last journey across the Broomway and he's desperate to never return. It should have taken him less than two hours to make it back to Wakering Stairs, but it feels like he's been wandering in the fog and the muck for days. He hadn't wanted to come back to the small town, and once there he'd been desperate to leave. Now the promise of the tide hangs over him, and the offer to spend the night in the barkeep's spare room suddenly seems more palatable. He wishes he'd accepted it.

———

The house was nearly exactly as he had remembered it: stone walls greyed by time, tattered wooden shingles, dirty glass windows, and acres of land now riddled with weeds. The only thing different about it was the neglect that had weaved itself through every crack of the property, like vines of ivy growing through a brick wall. Once the paperwork had been finalized, deed handed over, and the money exchanged, the only thing left for Edgar to do had been to leave. Which, as everyone on Foulness Island knew, he was especially good at. In truth, if it hadn't been for the farm losing value with each passing month it was left abandoned, he'd have never gone home.

———

HE INHALES DEEPLY, the salty air stinging his nostrils and making his eyes water, and he tries to recall if the Broomway normally smells so strongly of the sea, or if it's just the encroaching water. Edgar takes another step, but his foot plunges deep into the mud, throwing him off balance, and he falls to the ground as pain shoots up his leg. The papers in his jacket pocket spill out around him, grime and water saturating the paper and making the ink bleed.

———

DURING THEIR CORRESPONDENCE, Simon had insisted on leaving the door to the house unlocked after its sale, in case Edgar wanted to collect any of his things. He'd protested at first, writing back that any belongings he'd have wanted would have been collected by now. However, as the day of his trip neared, he was increasingly thankful Simon had insisted on opening the farmhouse to him one last time. The closer the sale got, the more palpable Edgar's pangs of grief had gotten at the thought of his old life, and the family that had once been the centre of it. While there weren't any photographs to collect or valuables to salvage, there had been comfort in the idea of revisiting the trinkets from a time long since past, and finally laying to rest the memories of his wife and his son.

———

HE WIPES his chin and the side of his face clean with the back of his hand, trying to remove as much of the sludge from his skin as he can, spitting some out as it runs into his open mouth. It's acrid and thick, and it makes him gag. He pushes himself up, tries to stand, and sits down just as fast. His ankle feels hot under his skin, like there's liquid metal running through his veins, and he whispers a silent prayer that he hasn't broken anything. The idea of making the long journey back to Bury St. Edmunds, even on horseback, will be especially daunting and equally unpleasant if he's broken a bone.

The fog presses in around him, kissing the back of his neck and chilling him through his wool clothes. His trousers are soaked through from his seat on the ground, and he suspects he'll need more than just one hot bath to clean the mud from his skin. Despite it being mid-afternoon, the sky is dark and the sun is entirely hidden behind curtains of grey. It fills him with dread as he imagines the approach of the water, at first trickling in, and then finding him all at once with great sweeping waves. *Is this what they wondered too?*

———

THE DOOR HANDLE was freezing cold against his sweaty palm, and once inside the house it was only a short walk to his old bedroom. A broken window by the kitchen confirmed what he'd already suspected; the place had been picked clean of any useful possessions. Still, Edgar made his way to the small bedroom he'd once shared with his late wife. The room was so much darker without Flora's smile to brighten it. Her blonde ringlets had made her appear cherubic even as an adult, and her blue eyes had been like endless summer skies. She had been soft, tender, and kind, and had loved him dearly. While their belongings had mostly been taken by those in need, some of her clothing had been left behind and strewn across the floor. He lifted a skirt to his face and breathed deep, the dust irritating his lungs and making him cough. But the smell of sweet clover was still there, however faint.

Not far from his bedroom was the nursery Joseph had slept in. He'd been a small baby, but had burgeoned into a big toddler and had been quickly outgrowing his crib. The wooden horse he'd played with and a few of his toy blocks were still heaped in the corner near where he'd slept. His crib, plain by any standard, was gone with the rest of his things. Edgar picked up the horse and rubbed his thumb across its long neck, removing a stripe of dirt and grime from the carved maple.

Joseph had tried to bring it with him on their trip to the market, but Flora had insisted he leave it behind. She'd worried he was going to lose it in the city and cry for a new one, which would have forced Edgar to spend money he didn't have on a toy his son didn't need.

She hadn't known it would be their final trip across the Broomway.
Edgar had.

———

HE TRIES to jerk his foot from the mud, but any movement at all sends a jolt of pain up his leg. He digs into the cold ground around his ankle, shovelling handfuls of wet earth away from his body in the hopes of getting himself loose, but it only makes things worse. With each scoop it feels like his leg is being dragged further in. He reaches down and tries to feel for the rim of his boot, hoping to grab the leather and tug his limb out, no matter how much it might hurt. But as he roots around the tender joint he doesn't feel the cowhide at all.

What he does feel sends a chill up his spine.

———

HE'D LOADED *the handcart with wheat, baked goods, preserves, and jars of honey. Flora was good at making jams and pickling food, and it was this skill that always guaranteed her more honey than her family could eat come fall. Edgar made sure the family kept only the smallest amount for themselves, and took the rest to the mainland to sweeten trades or turn a profit.*

Edgar had never been poor, and so he'd always had great hopes for himself and his life. With the house and inheritance from his father's passing—his mother long since dead and in no need of financial support—he'd never felt the burden of having to provide. But then he'd seen Flora, and her eyes blue like the heavens, and she was pregnant before they'd even had time to consider marriage. It was hard finding work with a soured reputation and few practical skills, and so he soon began farming the land he'd promised he'd leave. On the day of his son's birth he'd cried, mourning the life he'd wanted and the one he now had.

But it wasn't too late for him to start over.

It was a cold day the morning they left the farm, with fog thicker than cotton. Joseph was bundled in heavy wool, and Flora wore a long green cloak. He made sure they left later than planned, complaining about repairs that couldn't wait and misplacing his sheepskin gloves. By the time they left, he knew the tide wouldn't be far behind them. He led the way, pulling the handcart through the tall grass and over uneven roads. Joseph giggled from the back of it, sitting on the cart's wooden floor and watching as his mother brought up the rear of their three-person caravan. They waved goodbye to their neighbours, most of whom they'd seen in church on Sunday, and began their trek across the water.

Edgar always hated crossing the Broomway. A thin strip of land only visible when the tide was low, it was a road that had claimed more than its fair share of lives. It wasn't an overly long journey from the Foulness to the main- land, but it could be a hard one depending on the load he was hauling and the speed he was moving. The mud, stones, sand, and uneven footing made it hard to keep a brisk pace and made the handcart feel fifty pounds heavier. Sometimes the wheel would sink deep into the mud and become immovable, and so Edgar had quickly gotten into the habit of traveling with a plank of wood and a small spade in case he needed to liberate the cart from deep in the ground.

Except this time.

This time he left his tools at home, and when the wheel got stuck there was no way to free it.

HE SCREAMS, pushing backwards in the muck with all his might as he tries to wrench his leg free to no avail. The pain makes him breathless and spots appear in his vision. The fog trembles around him and he feels the... *thing* move up his leg. It grabs at him with hands as cold as ice. He's not sure if whatever has found him is trying to drag him under or if it's trying to pull itself out.

The form grabs at Edgar, moving faster, pulling its small body out of the mire. Too stunned to move, he watches as black eyes search his face and a pale, lipless mouth opens, rasps and gurgles spilling out from its throat. It grabs at him, clawing at his shirt. While its hands pass through the material of his sweater like air, they press down into his flesh and hold him in place.

Something moves behind him.

―――――

*H*E TOLD *them it was faster to run to the mainland and back than it was to go back to the Foulness. Flora asked to go with him, or at least for him to take Joseph, but he insisted they guard the handcart. All of their wares were on it, and if anyone stole them before they could bring them to market, they'd be done for, come winter. He needed them to wait for him. He promised he'd come back with help.*

She told him she would.

He could hear the lie in his words the moment he said them. He knew it wouldn't be long until the tide rushed in and washed them away. Soon he'd be free to start a new job, in a new town, in a new life of his own making. He kissed Flora goodbye, letting himself get lost in her eyes one final time, before running as fast as his feet could take him.

By the time he reached Wakering Stairs, he was soaked to the bone and nearly drowned.

It was more than he could say for his family.

―――――

EDGAR LOOKS over his shoulder to see the ground rising. *No, not the ground,* he realizes with some trepidation. Something coming out of the ground. It rises out of the mud, hovering over patches of coarse sand and moving silently through rocks, making its way towards him. This spectre is larger than the first and it looks through him with summer blue eyes.

He covers his mouth with his hands, muffling a scream.

Joseph presses the side of his face into his father's chest as Flora draws closer. He watches as she peels back her lips, fog pouring out and falling into clouds around her and cascading down the front of her gown as she tries to talk. The air rattles, but no sound is made.

The ground around Edgar is wet, and he wonders how long he's been stuck here, trying to free himself and outrun the tide. The smell of salt is heavier now and the sky above him looks nearly black.

Frantically, he tries to push Joseph off of him, but his hands pass clean through. They hurt, like they've been dunked in ice water, and

Edgar shouts desperately for help. He thrashes in the muck, drops of dirt splattering his face.

He hears Flora before he sees her, the heaving of her breath chilling him to the bone. She crouches next to him and wraps one arm across his chest, then snakes the other hand around his neck, her presence cold as ice and anchoring him alone to the ground. She rests the side of her head against the top of his shoulder, looking up at him as mud and tears trail down his sweater. She whispers again, but he doesn't understand.

The water rushes around him, moving fast and getting faster. He struggles against Flora and Joseph, who only hold him tighter. He tries to pull his leg from the earth, but with each attempt he sinks deeper. He shivers from the cold of both the Thames Estuary and his dead family. He knows it's a hopeless fight as the water quickly rises above his neck and forces its way down into his lungs. He turns his head and looks into his wife's blue eyes one last time.

He'd asked them to wait for him. His family had obliged.

IN OBEISANCE PARK

IF IT WASN'T FOR THE RED ON THE SAILS PEEKING OUT FROM THE waters of the mossy pond, Tucker never would have found the ship. Obeisance Park, which had once been the pride of the community, had long been abandoned by visitors and the city alike.

When the car factory had shut down almost twenty years ago and all the jobs had left, so too had the residents and most of the municipality's budget. And so Obeisance Park had been left to its own devices. The trees had grown tall and unruly, the grass long and untamed. Wildflowers had sprouted across the footpaths and out of their manicured beds, and the pond—now shielded from the sun thanks to the dense foliage around it, and without a caretaker to keep the algae at bay—had grown dark and mossy.

And it is in this state of ruin that Tucker, having spontaneously decided to take a shortcut home through the park, had discovers the boat drowned in the water.

Pulling a stick off a nearby tree, unconcerned about any authorities lecturing him about property damage, he leans over the stony edge of the water. The rocks have been deliberately arranged to look as natural as possible, but there is still something painfully obvious about their construction, much like the park itself. The now-wild greenspace has always felt artificial in the sea of grey apartment complexes and brick homes. He pushes the boat with the stick, trying to free it from the Creeping Jenny that spreads across the water and climbs up the stone. He pushes the boat again, harder now, accidentally catching part of the sail on the sharp wood and ripping a tear in the fabric.

Tucker curses under his breath, thankful his mom is still working at the grocery store and not within earshot of his foul language, and prods the boat with the stick once more. This time, he manages to loosen the green leaves from the mast of the ship, his heart beating with excitement as the front of the boat rises from the water. He reaches out to try and grab it from the dark water, but his arm isn't long enough. Although he's just started middle school, he looks like he could fit in comfortably with a class of fourth graders. His mom keeps telling him he'll grow into his age, that he'll shoot up like a string bean before he knows it.

"Everything in its time," she tells him whenever he comes home sulking, "even you."

He manages to hook the stick through the bowsprit and figurehead of the ship and dredges it from the mire. The smell hits him even before the state of it does. Somehow, the ship reeks worse than the forgotten pond, and Tucker wrinkles his nose in repulsion. It smells like rot and decay, like old meat left in the sun, and he imagines it must be the rotten wood of the hull. He leans back and sits on the overgrown grass by the end of the water, and sets the boat down on the ground in front of him, leaning it upright against one of the rocks. It looks slimy from the pond scum, and the last thing he wants is for his mom to get mad when he comes home smelling like dirty water, so he continues to prod the vessel with the tree branch.

He recognizes the boat, sort of, from history class. It looks like the great British galleons from the text book he'd been forced to read for homework and in the classes he tried not to sleep through. The sails, which had once been white, are muddied and browned by dirt. On the stern is a red flag with a St. George's cross in the top-left corner, the Colonial Ensign of the British. On the quarter gallery is intricately carved floral detailing and the whittled form of a woman draped in silks mounted on its exterior. Across the hull are holes ripped into the wood, as if the miniature ship had also endured battle alongside the rest of the royal navy.

The amount of detail on the toy surprises Tucker. It looks less like a child's plaything and more like a model he'd see with his class on a field trip to a museum far away, or one of the impressive creations kept in glass bottles, like the one his grandfather had displayed on his mantle above the fireplace. Everything from the tight slats of wood on the deck to the cloth sails, not to mention the remains of the standing rigging and stays, screams of expert craftsmanship even to a child as young as him.

He leans in closer from his seat in the grass, wanting to get a better look, when something moves inside the galleon. At first he thinks he's imagined it, but then he sees it again behind the opening of a gun hole, and Tucker's heart nearly stops in his chest. He's not sure what it is— *Do bugs even live in ponds?*—but he's startled when it scuttles from somewhere behind the wood again.

He's tempted to abandon the boat and go home, but the thought of going through the effort to clear the ship from the muck is enough to make him stand his ground. As much as he hates bugs, he hates letting them ruin his day even more. He takes the branch and loops it under one of the sails, jostling the ship and hoping to spill the waterbug from one of the small openings. Liquid sloshes out of the bottom of the boat, but the insect remains inside. He gives it another hard shake, but he only manages to tear the already-damaged sail further. He groans, resigned to clear the ship of its unwanted occupant, and tosses the branch to the side. While he doesn't want his mom angry at him for smelling like the pond, he doesn't see another way to shake the insect free. So, with an annoyed exhale, he reaches across the mud and grabs the boat, ready to shake it violently.

But he doesn't get a chance.

With a small pop, the ground is sucked out from under him, his vision blurs at the edges, and Tucker finds himself lying supine on a wet floor. He sits up and looks around, confused. The wood is dark and stained with green. It's slick to the touch and he falls to his knees a few times before he manages to get to his feet. Wood slats extend around him in every direction, fenced in by wooden taffrail to keep him from falling overboard. Above him stand the sails, their stained and putrid fabric reaching tall into the sky. The British ensign hangs lips and wet at the back of the galleon, the cool breeze too gentle to stir the sails.

He's on the boat.

Something stirs beneath the deck, footsteps getting louder as they climb the ladder to the upper gun deck. A hatch opens and a face looks out at him, eyes wide and sunken in. Tucker screams and tries to run, but only manages to slip and fall onto his back, his heart keeping pace with the man's quick steps towards him. The man looks down at him and Tucker realizes why the boat smelled like rotting flesh.

The man is old, his grey beard hanging halfway down his chest. What little hair he has atop his head is scraggly and damp, and it hangs to the centre of his back. His skin is profoundly wrinkled and a ghoulish grey, hints of blue and pink peeking out between sections where the skin has sloughed off entirely. His eyes are sunken in and white, his body bloated and near rupturing. His trunk hose and doublet are tight like casing on a sausage, his hanging sleeves covered in algae and mud. His mouth looks like a garish wound, red lips framing rotting teeth, water spilling over his chin and onto Tucker's chest as he stands over him and coughs.

"Are you the one the boat calls to?" he rasps. "If she has sung to you, then you have nothing to fear."

"Wh... what?"

"Have you been sent to free us from this bondage? From this hell?"

"I don't understand," Tucker says through his tears, teeth chattering from the cold dampness of the ship, wanting desperately to go home. "Who are you? Where am I? Why am I h-h-here?"

The man leans down and grabs the front of Tucker's shirt with a bony hand, flesh stripped from the back of the palm. What nails he still has are black from the water. He pulls the boy to his feet and draws him close, breathing on his face, the rotten flesh from inside his mouth putrid.

"We men waited for word from the King. Day and night we waited in the water, faithful, willing." From beneath the hull, hollow and voiceless screams of assent rise up. "But the food ran short and the storms raged, and we were left to die. We needed to make it to port, to safety, and then we found it. Hy-Brasil, west of Ireland, the island seen but once every seven years. We knew it was cursed, but what were we to do?"

The man lets go of Tucker's shirt and takes hold of his wrist, fingers digging into his flesh. He drags the boy behind him, rotting boots squelching on the half-deck as he pulls Tucker up the stairs leading to the ship's wheel.

"The witch trapped us here and made us small, hoping the ocean would swallow us whole. She abandoned us to time, to the water, to fate, until the one the ship calls to would lead us from the storm and steer us to safe harbour." The man pushes Tucker to the wheel, pointing at him with a blackened nail as water runs from his nose and down his cheek. "You have been chosen. Now steer us to safe harbour."

"I-I-I don't know how. I've never done this. I don't know how."

"Steer us to safe harbour!" the man screams, his crewmates echoing his shouts below the hull. "Steer us to safe harbour! Or be damned with us!"

Tucker stumbles towards the wheel, his running shoes slipping on the wet wood of the deck. The wheel is covered in algae and muck, the floor thick with slime and pools of water. The man watches him, eyes wide and fixed, as Tucker reaches out and touches the wheel with one hand. Like metal to a magnet, his other hand is drawn to it, and he quickly finds himself stuck. At first nothing happens, and he stands there frozen, hands wrapped around the spokes.

Then comes the blistering pain that courses through his body like a live wire. He tries to scream, but he's frozen at the wheel. And then he feels it at the tip of his fingers, the change, the shift, the loss of his form. His hands, his arms, his entire body, melts into a pool of water. It spills over the wheel, pouring out on the deck around the wheel, bleeding into the water and mire of those sucked in before him.

With a deep sigh the man turns back and heads to the ladder that brings him into the hull.

"Not the one."

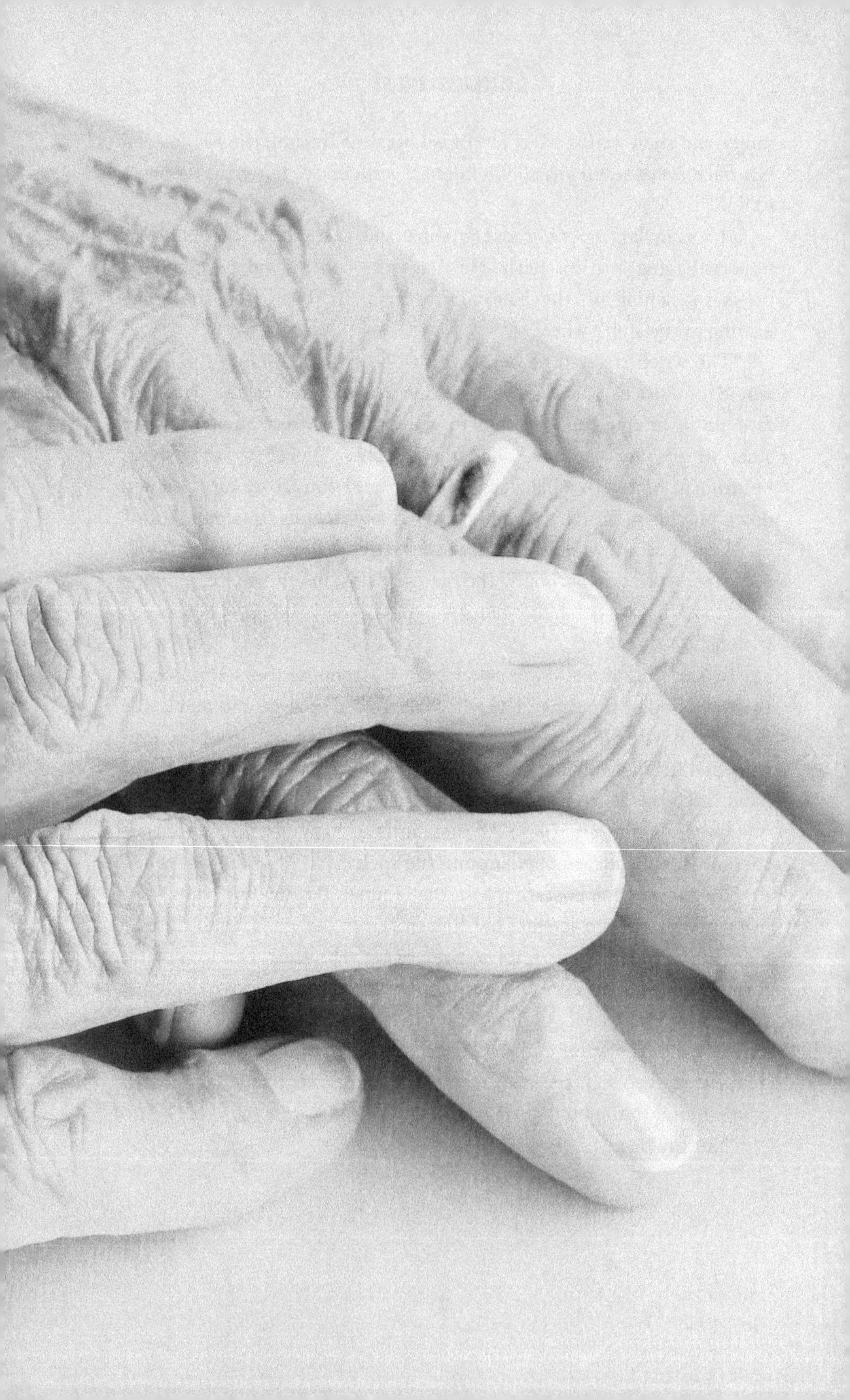

GORDON

The door to Penny's apartment closes with a dull thud, and she clicks the lock into place with a bony hand. A large cardboard box and a cage made of plastic and metal rest on the beige carpet nearby. She shuffles to her kitchen, grabs one of the small wooden chairs arranged around a matching table, and drags it slowly behind her as she makes her way back to the entrance. She takes a seat, knees cracking with age as she makes herself comfortable, and she silently thanks her friend for encouraging her to join the water aerobics class at the nearby rec centre. *You might be old, but you're not dead*, her friend had joked. She drags the carrier close and leans down, looking into it.

Two bright green eyes look back at her.

"Well, aren't you just the most handsome little man," she coos.

The ginger tabby watches her from the back of the cage, his tail wrapped around his body protectively, his eyes wide and cautious. Around his neck is a green collar, the same shade as his eyes, and from it hangs a circular silver tag. Penny is sure something is engraved on it but she is unable to read it without her glasses.

She sticks a finger between the bars for the cat to smell. She's only ever had dogs before now and is unsure how to introduce herself to the small animal. Should she pet it? Let it get her scent? Release it into the apartment with reckless abandon? She settles on trying to convince the cat she's not a threat, and hopes he won't find her scent offensive or cause to bite her. He stares wide-eyed at her while she waits patiently for him to approach her hand and decide whether or not she's a danger to him. It's a long time before he finally moves closer, and when he does he wastes no time in rubbing the side of his face against her outstretched finger, marking her with his scent and purring heavily.

"Oh, what a sweet little boy. And so brave, too," she coos, unlocking the carrier and opening it a little wider for him. Before she can put her hand in, he pushes his way out and begins rubbing his face against her legs, weaving in and out as she pets his golden fur. He purrs, the noise deep and soothing, and she smiles when he flings himself onto his back and lets her rub his tummy. Once he's satisfied with his belly rubs, he rolls back onto his paws and jumps in her lap. He watches her like he's trying to get a good look at her face, and then gives her a few tender slow blinks. She smiles back at the little cat, kissing the top of his forehead. Her attention is drawn to the collar around his neck and the silver tag that hangs from it, and she turns the nameplate towards her.

GORDON.

She inhales sharply, her chest tight with emotion, and kisses the cat on the top of his head once more. He licks his shoulder and jumps off her lap, seemingly satisfied that Penny's no danger. He trots off to explore the apartment while she gets up, makes her way to the small kitchen counter, and picks up her cordless phone. She looks at the post-it taped to the back of the device, locates her son's name from the list, and dials the number as it's written next to the name. The buttons are stiff—or maybe it's just her arthritic fingers—and she tries to punch the numbers in quickly. The last time she tried to call Ron, she took so long to dial that the phone kept trying to call out before she'd finished entering the number. It rings a few times before a man picks up on the other end.

"Hello?"

"Ron," she says, "was this you?"

"Hey, Mom! Was what me?"

"Gordon!"

"Oh, yes! He arrived today?"

"Oh, sweetie, he's such a cute little thing. And when I saw he had your father's name—" she stops, choking up.

"I'm glad you like him, Mom."

"I love him. Where did you find him? And how the heck did you get him here? You and the kids aren't set to visit for another month."

"Well, it's actually not a very exciting story. Do you remember Todd?"

"Todd?"

"Yeah, he was Mary's boy, lived down the street from us. Cheryl and I were best friends with him and we've always kinda kept in touch."

"Oh! Oh my goodness, it's been so long since I've heard that name. Mary, she was always such a nice woman. How's she doing?"

"She passed away, Mom. Remember? It's been a few years now."

"Oh. I must have forgotten, sorry."

"It's okay. Well, anyway, he had a younger sister who recently passed away. She didn't have any kids or anything, so Todd was the one who had to go clear out her belongings in the seniors' home she lived at. It turns out she had a cat—apparently, it had belonged to this guy in the building who would just stare at people, his name was like George or Geoffrey or whatever—and it had been living alone in the apartment for almost a week."

"The poor thing must have been so frightened!"

"I can imagine. So Todd takes the little guy with her, but he couldn't keep him because of the dogs, so he offered him to me. But you know how my allergies can get, not to mention Rebecca's at that stage where she tries to put everything in her mouth and can be rough without meaning to be, so I told him I couldn't take him. And then he told me his name and how his wife was going to be in your neck of the woods this week and I just knew it was a sign that he should be with you. Besides, I know you've been lonely lately, what with Dad gone and Maggy and me down south for work, so I thought this was a good idea. I hope it was, anyways. I know I should have asked you ahead of time if you wanted a cat, but—"

"He's perfect, Ron. Absolutely perfect."

"I'm glad. So, for our next visit up there, I was thinking—no,

Rebecca, you put that down right now! I'm so sorry, Mom, but I have to go. She's got her hands on the—I said this instant! Bye, love you, Mom!"

Before Penny can reply, the other line goes quiet with a click.

She smiles to herself as she puts the receiver down. Ron had been like that growing up; a tornado with legs. He'd rip things off the table you didn't even know were there, then send them flying across the room. And when he seemed like he'd finally tuckered himself out, he'd surprise you with a second wind, only this time everything he touched he tried to stuff in his mouth. Penny had been surprised when Maggy had announced her pregnancy a couple of short years ago. She and Ron had always said they wanted to have children later in life, but after Ron's fortieth birthday Penny had assumed they'd decided against children altogether. But lo and behold, shortly after his forty-first, they'd announced that Maggy was pregnant.

Penny makes her way around the counter to the chair and drags it back to its spot at the table. She then sets up the litter box in the bathroom—grateful that she's been given the lightweight kind—and then brings some of the toys that were left for Gordon out to the living room. At the sound of the bells jingling in the tweed mice, the ginger tabby comes jogging out from his exploration of her bedroom. She takes a seat on her La-Z-Boy, slipping on her slippers, and pulls out one of the mice. She shakes the toy and he stares at it, wide-eyed and eager. She throws it into the middle of the living room and watches as he chases after it, pouncing on the mouse and jumping around with it between his teeth. Satisfied he's killed the tweed beast, he brings it back to her and spits it onto the carpet. He purrs, rubbing himself on her shin until she pets him. He arches his hindquarters as she scratches the fur at the base of his tail, pressing into her hand as she pets him. When he's satisfied he pulls away and sits down, pawing at the toy and mewling. She picks it up again and gives it another toss.

Gordon runs across the carpet and pounces on the mouse, running away, and circling back to pounce on it again. He chews on it, runs away again, and then picks it up in his mouth. He runs past Penny and stops at the entranceway to her bedroom, spitting the toy onto the ground and looking up at the air. He paws at it, mewling once more, eyes fixed on the empty doorway. He arches his back and stands fixed in one spot, purring, before throwing himself onto his back. He stays there, wriggling on the carpet until Penny finally gets up from her seat and hobbles to him.

"Silly boy, you have to bring it to me. Otherwise, I can't throw it for you."

She picks up the toy and walks back to her chair with it. Once seated, she throws the mouse and he runs after it, playing with her like this well into the afternoon. Once Gordon is tired of running, he curls up in her lap and the two of them enjoy their afternoon nap together.

SHE WAKES UP WITH A START.

The apartment is pitch black and her neck hurts. She realizes, with some surprise, that she's still in her recliner with Gordon curled up in her lap. She leans over and turns on the lamp on the coffee table beside her, squinting at the sudden bright light that engulfs the room. The clock on the wall says it's after ten, meaning she's slept for almost six hours, and yet somehow she's still tired. She looks around, freezing, when something moves in her peripheral vision. She looks over her shoulder in time to catch what looks like something moving into her bedroom. She gets to her feet, unceremoniously dumping the cat onto the carpet, and shuffles to the kitchen as fast as her bad hips can take her. She picks up the cordless phone off its charger and pushes the ON button, a finger poised above the keypad and ready to dial 9-9-9 at a moment's notice.

She moves from the kitchen and through the living room, stepping carefully around the carpet. The last thing she needs now is to trip and fall, not when someone could be in her bedroom. Her heart is hammering against her ribs and she hasn't felt this afraid since her husband's stroke. She tries to move quietly, knowing it's foolhardy to think catching a burglar by surprise will somehow give her any real advantage, but she finds it a hard task to accomplish. As she nears the doorway she shuffles faster, the hair standing up on the back of her neck.

She bursts into the room, finger pre-emptively dialling 9, but finds the room empty. She flicks on the light switch by the door and steadies herself on the doorframe, blood pumping in her ears and lightheaded from the stress.

The room is empty.

She walks around the space, taking the time to open her closet door and even getting onto her knees to check underneath the bed. Satisfied that no one's in the room with her, she holds onto the bed frame to help pull herself up and puts the phone back in the kitchen. Gordon brushes himself against her leg, chirping, and soon all worries about break-ins are forgotten as Penny concerns herself with feeding her new best friend.

———

IT'S NOT her alarm that wakes her the next morning, but Gordon shifting his weight as he sleeps on her chest, purring against her ribs. His paw digs uncomfortably into her breast and she tries to shift him into a more manageable position. He doesn't fuss when she pushes him to the middle of her chest, instead closing his eyes and continuing to sleep. She rubs the top of his head, running a bony knuckle along the bridge of his nose to between his ears. He looks so comfortable, curled up on top of her bed covers with a paw tucked under his chin, and she envies his ability to sleep in. She looks around the room, trying to figure out how early it must be. Her alarm still hasn't gone off but the room is already aglow with morning light streaming in from the curtains, which were left partially open when she fell asleep.

She turns to look at the small alarm clock on her nightstand, trying her best not to disturb the sleeping cat while craning her neck to get a good look at the glowing green numbers.

12:34 P.M.

She frowns and pulls herself closer to the alarm clock.

12:34 P.M.

"That's impossible."

She picks Gordon up and moves him onto the bed beside her, then rolls onto her side and pushes herself up into a seated position. Her bones hurt, back stiff and joints creaking in protest under her paper-thin skin, as she gets herself up to sitting on the edge of the queen-sized bed. She picks the clock up and flips it over, her frown deepening when she finds that the switch for her alarm is still set to ON. She pushes herself to her feet and shuffles slowly across the cold floor of the bedroom to her closet, which she opens to retrieve a housecoat from, before draping the cloth around her thin frame and making her way into the living room.

She checks the clock on the wall, hoping that maybe there's a problem with the alarm in her bedroom. It's old, after all, and the batteries haven't been changed in some time. Maybe the clock has stopped working and is frozen on the time it died? Or maybe the alarm says it's set to ON, but the switch is defective?

12:35 P.M.

She makes her way into the kitchen, sliding her feet into her slippers by the La-Z-Boy as she walks past, and puts on a pot of coffee. She fills the water receptacle and empties the old coffee grounds from the mesh basket, filling it with new ones from the canister she keeps on the counter. It doesn't make sense that she's so tired, especially with the nap she took yesterday, not to mention the early bedtime last night. Although she might still be sleepy from oversleeping, it doesn't explain why her joints are painful and raw, like they've been over-worked in their cartilage-less sockets.

As the coffee percolates, she makes her way to her medicine cabinet in the bathroom to take her morning medications. She squeezes her inhaler, breathing the medication in deep, and cringes as her finger cracks and pops. Her hands are sore and the skin is sensitive, and it makes opening her pill bottles an exercise in both patience and pain management. She turns on the faucet and fills a paper cup with water, then pops the pills all at once and washes them down. She splashes some of the cool water onto her face, warm from the hours spent under her comforter with the added heat of Gordon, and uses the hand towel to dry off. She feels the familiar warmth of fur against her leg and the cat's deep purrs, and she reaches a hand down to stroke his head before slowly standing upright and looking at herself in the mirror.

A second set of green eyes looks back at her.

She shrieks, dropping the towel and scaring Gordon out of the bathroom, as she turns quickly to look behind her. The eyes were staring at her from the shower, but there's nothing in the tub but her washcloth and plastic bottles. She looks over her shoulder into the mirror, but the only eyes staring back at her now are own her wide ones. She lets out a shaky exhale, pressing a cold hand against a flushed cheek, before picking the towel up off the floor and returning it to its hook on the side of the vanity.

The phone rings and she jumps, still reeling from the imaginary eyes in the mirror. She crosses the apartment to the kitchen, picks the phone off the charger, and answers.

"Hello?"

"Mom! Hey, how was your first night with Gordon? Are you two getting along?"

"Oh, yes! He's perfect. We spent the night cuddling," she says, balancing the receiver between her ear and shoulder as she takes a coffee cup out of the cabinet and puts it on the counter. Even though the coffee pot isn't full, it takes her two hands to pour the hot liquid into the mug and replace the pot back onto its burner.

"Oh, that's nice! I'm glad he's working out with you so far!"

"He's perfect."

Penny spoons in some sugar and adds a splash of cream to her cup while Ron talks about work and his family. Although the two of them spend the rest of the hour catching up, she never mentions the eyes in the mirror.

————

AROUND FOUR, Penny decides to be a bad cliche and makes herself an early supper (or, as she tries to convince herself, an exceptionally late lunch). Her eyes have been heavy all day, and despite her medication for her arthritis pain, she's still hurting all over. While she'd originally had plans to take the bus to the shops and then pass by the bank, she can't bring herself to do anything that requires much effort. She spends most of the day in her recliner either playing fetch with Gordon or petting him while he's curled up on her lap. She nearly fell asleep the last time he decided to climb up on her, waking with a start when she suddenly felt like she was falling through ice, and decided that more coffee and maybe some food would do her well.

She stands in front of the stove as the eggs fry in the pan, lids heavy as she watches them cook. She stirs the beans in the pot with a spoon and puts the bread in the toaster, waiting until everything is nearly done before pressing the lever and heating the slices of rye. Gordon weaves between her feet, chirping as she busies herself with the food. He mewls at her for attention, trotting towards his food bowl by the refrigerator when she looks down to see what he wants.

"Oh, so you're hungry too, eh? You're not supposed to eat it all so quickly, you cheeky boy."

She picks up his bowl and moves to the pantry, where she takes out the dental food, opening the resealable bag and scooping some into his dish. She closes the bag and returns it to the pantry before bending over to put the bowl back. As she leans against the fridge for support and lowers his dish to the ground a chill runs up her spine, her heart beating in her ears.

Someone is standing beside her.

Her breath catches in her chest, eyes watering reflexively as she holds the bowl an inch above the ground, terrified to move. The person stands close enough that she can make out their legs—brown loafers and navy trousers—but can't see much else about them. Unfortunately, while she can't make out what they look like, she can hear their heavy wheezing from above her. They inhale slowly; the noise is awful and wet and sounds like it's coming from deep in their throat. They exhale just as slow, the noise like someone trying to force air out of a wet straw.

She sets the dish on the ground and Gordon trots happily over, seemingly unaware (or at least unconcerned) about the stranger standing over them. Penny grips the door of the fridge tighter and pulls herself to her feet as quickly as she can, the muscles in her back clenching and spasming from the suddenness of her movement. She turns as fast as her body will allow, ready to grab the pan off the stove and swing it wildly in self-defence, but finds herself alone in the kitchen, with the exception of Gordon at her feet. She looks around wildly, trying to find where the person went, but she's alone in her apartment. She leans against the stove, breathing fast and struggling to draw in air.

She makes her way to the bathroom, opens the medicine cabinet, and takes out her inhaler. She can smell the eggs burning from across the apartment, but she doesn't care; there are bigger concerns right now. She gives the plastic actuator a quick shake, her medical alert bracelet jingling on her wrist, and closes her eyes as she presses the canister and inhales through the mouthpiece.

Behind her, someone gives a great rattling wheeze, their breath on the back of her neck.

She opens her eyes and stares into the mirror, green eyes peering back.

She screams and runs for the phone in the kitchen. She knows she won't be able to outrun whoever's in here with her, and she prays they won't bother chasing her through her home. She makes her way through the living room, the kitchen counter in sight. As she extends a hand, reaching out for the phone, her slipper catches on the rug and she crashes to the ground with a shout.

Her leg is on fire from the hip down and she can't move it. She starts to cry, great heaving sobs, and Gordon rushes to her side to see what's wrong. She tries to drag herself into the kitchen, but she doesn't have the strength to do anything more than roll onto her back as she looks for the intruder.

Smoke from the kitchen burns her eyes. She can hear the hiss of the eggs burning and charring in the pan and the bubbling of the tomato sauce and beans on the stove. Gordon climbs on top of her chest and looks down at her with his bright green eyes, blinking slowly at her. He flattens his ears against his head as the smoke alarm blares overhead, and Penny wraps her arms around him as she waits for help to arrive.

———

PENNY PRETENDS to be asleep as the doctor and Ron talk on the other side of the curtain that divides her portion of the hospital room from the space designated for the other patient and their family, as well as their joint bathroom. She's hot in the face, embarrassed that her son had to fly out to see her in the hospital because of her carelessness, ashamed that she could have gotten other people hurt had her supper caught fire. But as upset as she is about the fall, the almost-fire, and the broken hip, she's mostly mad that nobody will believe that there was someone with her inside the apartment.

The fire department said her door was locked from the inside when they arrived, and they couldn't find any proof that someone had let themselves into her home, but she insisted she wasn't alone. She begged them to listen to her, trying to keep herself from hysterics as she explained how the eyes had been in her mirror that morning, how a shadow had run into her bedroom the night before, how the wheezing had followed her across the apartment.

They talk about her living situation and how it needs to change moving forward. Although Ron has already agreed to stay with his mother for the next two weeks following the hip replacement, the doctor stresses that the amount of follow-up care and supervision that Penny will need going forward is great enough that they should strongly consider having her moved to a seniors' centre.

The doctor worries about Penny's mental health, asking Ron if his mother has ever shown signs of dementia, or if there's a history of mental illness in the family. Ron tries to answer as candidly as he can, telling him that his grandmother died from Alzheimer's when he was still in school, how his mother has been dealing with isolation since her husband died and how Ron moving away has only compounded those feelings. He talks about how his mother has slowly been forgetting phone numbers and names, but he never thought it was abnormal. The doctor stresses the importance of monitoring Penny, and he recommends a care home again.

Penny closes her eyes, the morphine drip helping her fall back to sleep, and she sinks into uneasy dreams of wheezing cats and getting lost in a sea of smoke.

———

IT DOESN'T TAKE LONG for Penny to get settled into her new home. Or, more accurately, it doesn't take Ron and the movers long to get her into her new home. There's little about the facility that interests her, but for the sake of Ron she smiles and feigns excitement when she's told all about the bowling alley and movie theatre and dance hall that she'll be able to use, but only "when you're up to it."

They like to throw that term around a lot. *When you're up to it.* Twice she's requested someone bring her a box of her belongings so she can help sort and organize her apartment in the facility to her liking, and twice they've told her not to worry and to focus on getting better.

"You can rearrange things later, Mom," Ron says firmly. He tells her not to fret as he folds things incorrectly and stuffs clothing into drawers that's meant to be hung up. "Who are you trying to impress in here, anyway?" he teases.

"It's bad enough that I'm stuck using a walker. Are you really going to trap me here and force me to wear wrinkled trousers?" Gordon purrs in her lap as she scratches his chin, eyes closed with contentment.

"You're not trapped in here, Mom, but be realistic. We both knew this day was coming, and with your hip on the mend it's the perfect time to move you in here. Besides, you always said you liked the look of this place, right? There are worse places you could live besides the Ridgeview."

"I know. I just... I miss my home."

"This *is* your home, Mom. You'll love it, I promise. Plus, it's in a great neighbourhood with top-notch security. They've got a guard downstairs and a sign-in counter for visitors. So nobody's going to get in here without an invitation," he says with a sad smile and a reassuring nod.

"You still don't think anyone was in the apartment with me." She doesn't phrase it like a question.

"Because there *wasn't* anyone in the apartment with you."

She knows there was, but doesn't want to push the issue. She spent the better part of the last two and a half weeks telling people she wasn't crazy, which has only helped convince everyone that she's mad. Although it's her first day being fully moved into the building, she's already had a consultation with the centre's psychiatrist and on-site physician, who've made it clear that they'll be checking in on her regularly—along with the team's nursing staff and physiotherapist—and that she can call them if she's feeling "distressed."

He closes her last dresser drawer and gets to his feet. He disassembles the box that had once held her clothing and puts it on the stack of flattened boxes by the bed. She watches him from her seat on the edge of the mattress as he tapes the cardboard together so he can carry it out of the home. His flight is in a few hours, and she knows if he doesn't leave soon that he'll miss his plane south for the night.

"This is for the best, Mom. You'll see. If anything happens, you can always call the front desk and they'll send someone up to check on you. If you fall or if there's an emergency, press the button we got you," he says, motioning to the alter necklace around her neck. "And remember that I'm only a phone call away if you want to chat or if you're feeling lonely. Although I doubt that'll be a problem thanks to Gordon here, not to mention all the social clubs this place has. Love you, Mom."

"I love you too, sweetie. Give Maggy and Rebecca my love, and call me when you land, okay?"

"Of course."

He gives Gordon a scratch behind the ears before leaning down and kissing his mom on the top of her head. He hugs her delicately, insisting that she not bother getting up to walk him to the door, then takes the cardboard boxes and leaves her apartment. The door to her unit closes with a soft click, locking automatically behind Ron.

Although the furniture in her new apartment has been arranged to look like her old one, there's a coldness to the space. Her last apartment had had robin's egg walls and dark wood flooring, not to mention her gorgeous (albeit dangerous) beige shag carpet in the living room. This apartment feels sterile and void of life, with white walls and white wall-to-wall carpeting, designed to soften falls better than hardwood while being short enough not to trip seniors or get mobility aids stuck in the pile.

Gordon jumps off her lap, chirping as he walks to the end of the bed and arches his back. He stays like that for a while before throwing himself onto the floor and wriggling onto his back. Penny smiles at him, glad her son was able to find a private long-term care home that accepts cats, and laughs as he gets to his feet and walks figure-eights at the foot of her bed. Eventually, he jumps back onto the mattress next to her, purring against her thigh.

The exhaustion of the day is finally catching up to her and she feels more drained than she did in the hospital following her surgery. She tells herself an early night is just what the doctor ordered, and since she's already in pyjamas the idea looks even better than it did a moment ago. Carefully, she holds onto her walker and gets off the bed, rearranges the covers the way she likes them, and gets back into it. Gordon curls up on the pillow next to her, and she drifts to sleep.

———

WHEEZING.

Wet, strangled, laboured *wheezing*.

The sound of it gets her heart pumping even before she's fully awake. It's the noise that pulls her from the emptiness at the back of her mind and sends her consciousness rocketing back into her body. She's suddenly very aware of her surroundings, and the knowledge that she's not alone makes her breath hitch in her chest. She hopes the person doesn't realize that she's awake.

The dread she feels is familiar and it envelops her, thick and heavy like tar. The Ridgeview Seniors' Home was supposed to be safe. They promised her she would be protected from intruders, that the security man at the door and the people at the check-in counter would prevent this from happening again. But as they breathe through their mouth, this wet sucking in of oxygen, it's clear that abandoning her home was all for naught.

How did they find me? she silently screams to herself.

Gordon purrs and begins to knead the comforter, shifting his weight back and forth, paw to paw, on her chest. She can feel his whiskers against her nose and the corner of her lips, and his comforting presence helps her not to panic as the realization of her situation sets in. She's alone in her bedroom with a stranger. No.

She's injured, immobile, and alone in her bedroom with a stranger.

She tries to steady her breathing and clear the panic from her mind.

Panic... the panic button!

She's suddenly acutely aware of the weight of the necklace, the metal chain warmed by her body pressing into her skin. She takes a deep breath, noticing how the button cuts into her breastbone as her body expands under the weight of the ten-pound cat. The situation is less than ideal—with one hand at her side and the cat atop the panic button—but far from hopeless. Her right hand rests on her stomach and she's hopeful that, so long as the person isn't right on top of her, she might be able to slide her hand up and press the switch.

Except she doesn't know where the person is.

With her heart hammering, she cracks her eyes open just wide enough to see through her eyelashes and into the dark. She hopes the room is dim enough that they can't tell she's awake. Her eyes take a second to adjust to the slivers of moonlight that filter in through the cracks in her curtains, but soon it's clear that the person isn't within her line of sight. She takes this as a sign to try moving, so she drags her hand slowly towards the necklace, moving it millimetre by millimetre across her body. She even manages to slide her hand under Gordon without him fussing, but it's only when her hands reach the smooth plastic that she realizes the wheezing has gotten louder.

No.

Closer.

It's then that she feels it, the breath against the side of her face, the face just outside of her field of vision. The person's been watching her this entire time, staring at her from her blind spot near the nightstand.

She doesn't know what compels her to look, but she gives up the pretence of faking sleep and turns her head to look at the figure.

Sunken green eyes stare back at her, his mouth hanging open on his gaunt face just inches from her own. He leans towards her and she screams, turning away from the unsettling visage as she throws a protective arm over the cat and presses the button on the alert necklace over and over as she shrieks. It only takes a few minutes before someone's at her door, forcing the key into the lock and barging through her apartment. A pair of nurses come running through to the bedroom, turning on the lights and seeing what's the matter.

Penny hardly notices them, her arms wrapped around Gordon, yelling at a face that's no longer there.

———

THE FOOD SITS on the table beside her, but she wants nothing to do with it. She's not hungry, she hasn't been for days, but the doctor is insisting she get food down. The medication they've put her on, Ziprasidone, constantly makes her stomach sore and makes her feel like she's going to throw up at a moment's notice. She feels tired all the time and has to take constant breaks during physiotherapy for her hip. She keeps telling them she doesn't like how the medication makes her feel, but they insist that she keep taking it. She tells them she's tired all the time, that it's harder to move, that her head is always pounding. They tell her that it's for her own good, that it'll help with the hallucinations, that it'll help her sleep.

And it does help her sleep. Penny thinks that's the one thing the medication *is* good for, since it's the only thing she seems to be able to do. Just getting out of bed long enough to feed Gordon is enough to relegate her to bed for a nap. It's in these moments, under the covers and all by herself, that she's especially grateful for her cat. Every time, without fail, he climbs onto her chest and purrs, lulling her to sleep with his gentle vibrations and calming noises. Gordon makes her feel less isolated, less scared, less trapped. He doesn't argue when she tells him what she saw that night. He doesn't dismiss her when she worries that she no longer feels like herself.

The doctors do, though, and so does Ron.

"It's for your own good, Mom," he tells her over the phone as she pulls the corner off a piece of cheese that is poking out of her sandwich and feeds it to Gordon. "This will help you get your head on straight so you can enjoy your twilight years. You want to enjoy them, don't you?"

"Yes, of course I do. But not like this. I'm not crazy."

"No one's saying you're crazy, Mom."

"You are. The doctors are."

"Nobody has ever said that you're crazy."

"You're all telling me that I didn't see anyone in my bedroom that night."

"No, we're telling you that you saw someone in your bedroom, but that nobody was there. Your brain is playing tricks on you, Mom, just like Nana's brain played tricks on her."

The memory of Penny's mother in her final months is a gut-punch. Her mother, towards the end of her life, couldn't remember who anyone was anymore. She couldn't understand that Penny was her daughter, or that she was even old enough to have a daughter. She kept begging the doctors to see her father and kept asking the hospital staff to let her go home, until one day she couldn't remember how to ask for anything properly. Words began to fade from her memory, and by the time she passed away, she couldn't even eat on her own. The idea of turning into her mother had terrified her well into retirement.

Now, the fact that no one believes she is still sane scares her even more.

"Look," Ron tells her through the phone, "I have to go pick up Maggy and Rebecca from their Mommy-and-Me playdate, but I'll call you tomorrow to see how you're doing. Love you, Mom."

Before she can find the energy to reply, he's hung up.

She looks at the sandwich on the plate and picks it up. She takes a small bite—teeth crunching through the mock-meat, cheese, and lettuce—and swallows the food, wishing almost immediately that she hadn't. The bread sticks to the back of her throat as it makes its way into her stomach, and the second it lands there she feels like heaving it back up. Deciding the sandwich isn't working, she picks up the metal fork, prods at a cube of cantaloupe from her fruit salad, and gets it down. This too is uncomfortable for her, stomach gurgling in revolt. Beads of sweat collect on the back of her neck and her face is flushed. She needs to lie down.

Too tired to be proper about it, she lets herself fall back onto the mattress, fork still gripped tightly in her hand. She stares at the ceiling and closes her eyes, blinking slowly.

When she opens them, the room is dark. Nighttime.

That's impossible, it's just after lunch.

She cranes her neck and looks at the alarm clock next to her.

7:42 P.M.

The bed sags next to her.

The man wheezes, struggling to inhale.

At first, the only thing Penny can hear is the blood rushing in her ears, but soon a horrible noise fills the apartment. A desperate, exhausted, low wail. It grows and expands, stretching on and on, and it's with horror that Penny realizes the sound is coming from her. She tightens her hold on the fork, the cold metal digging into her flesh, and she howls as she turns to look at the man next to her. He watches her, his green eyes empty and his mouth abstrusely wide, as he lounges on the bed. She stabs at the man, swinging the fork wildly. It's a colossal effort, her body weak and stiff, her bones sore and muscles aching, but she stabs at the man.

She doesn't notice the orderlies coming to restrain her, or the needle that's prepared for her when she slashes at a nurse. She only sees the man, green eyes and gaping mouth, and she keeps on fighting.

————

THE ROOM SPINS around her as she lies in the bed. Her chest is tight and her body is sore. She only just woke up and already she wants to go back to sleep. She tries to move her arms but they don't want to obey her brain, the drugs that were used to sedate her still in her system. Gordon lies on her chest and looks down at her, mewling when he sees she's awake.

"Hey, you," she whispers to him, smiling as he lowers his head close enough for her to kiss the top of it. "Who's my little man?"

Gordon stands up and stretches, then jumps off her chest and onto the ground. She watches as he walks in figure eights on the carpet beside the bed. The room feels colder and a chill runs up her spine as Gordon stops walking and purrs at the air. She watches as a pale bony hand runs its fingers through his ginger fur, the cat now arching his back and hindquarters to deepen the scratch. He throws himself onto his back and wriggles on the carpet as the man rubs his belly and coos at him. Once Gordon is satisfied with the attention, he gets back onto his feet, weaves between the man's legs a few more times, and jumps onto the bed with Penny. His paws dig uncomfortably into her flesh as he walks over her stomach and stands on her ribcage, before finally curling up on her chest.

The man approaches her, silently, shuffling across the carpet and sitting next to her on the edge of her bed. He pets Gordon, who looks up at him tenderly with his deep green eyes, and begins purring. Penny watches, terrified, as the man leans over her, his mouth open, and inhales deeply, wheezing. With each inhale he looks a little more solid. With each exhale she feels a little weaker.

She tries to scream for help, tries to beg someone—anyone—for help, but there's only wheezing.

———

R ON RUNS his hand over the cat's golden fur, petting him in the living room of his mother's Ridgeview apartment. Or, more accurately, what had once been her apartment. He'd known this day was coming since she broke her hip, but anticipating her death and experiencing it were two different things entirely. The cat is curled in his lap, purring, and a sense of calmness washes over him as he holds Gordon close. He wonders if the feline was at least some small comfort to his mother in her final moments.

His phone rings from inside his jacket pocket and he fishes it out, one hand still on the cat.

"Hello?"

"Hey, sweetie, how are things going over there?"

"I mean, as well as can be expected. She's being transferred to Cedar Heights, like we requested, although the secretary didn't seem to know what the hell she was doing."

"And what are you going to do with the cat? Are you taking him with you?"

"No, no. He's going to stay here. Apparently, a few of the residents have been looking for companion animals, and a bunch of them have already met Gordon through Mom, so the administration said they're going to keep him here and see how it goes. I told them that if it didn't work out, then we'd take him. Oh, they also wanted to know if—shit, can I call you back? The front desk is phoning me."

"Sure! Talk soon!"

Ron hangs up the phone and answers the other call, letting go of Gordon and pushing himself onto his feet. He smiles to himself as the cat walks figure-eights on the carpet, mewling at the air.

THE BLUE

THE TIRES CRUNCH OVER DIRT AND GRASS, FLATTENING DANDELIONS and anthills as the pickup truck makes its way closer to the water's edge, soft ground eventually giving way to hard flat stone. Reid unbuckles his seatbelt and opens the passenger door before his friend comes to a full stop.

"You're sure about this?" Thomas asks, putting the Ford in park.

"Yup!" he shouts, already out the door. "Why wouldn't I be?"

Thomas shakes his head, undoing his own safety belt and meeting his friend at the rear of the vehicle.

"I don't know, man. There's something about being alone on the water that freaks me out. What if you fall in? What if you get lost? How are you going to call anyone for help? You should at least bring your phone."

Reid laughs as he opens the trunk and steps into the box bed to unstrap his kayak and paddle.

"You worry too much! This river is calm and the lake it leads to is even calmer. If I fall in or take a swim, I don't want to ruin my phone. Just meet me back here in three hours," he says, checking his waterproof watch. "It's not like Kicking Horse River that'll kick your dick if you don't know what you're doing. Not that you'd know... you sure you don't want to come with me?"

"God, no."

"Still scared of the water, eh?"

Thomas shrugs and helps slide the kayak out of the truck. "I'm not scared, I just don't like it. There's a difference."

"Whatever you say."

"Why do you even want to go kayaking here? It's gotta be boring compared to the other places you've been."

"I don't know. I guess I've lived here all my life and I'm tired of taking this river for granted," Reid lies.

Once the thin blue boat is out of the pickup, Reid carries it to the water. He braces one end of the paddle across the back of the kayak and the other against the rocks. He grabs the pole and, using his upper body strength, maneuvers himself into the seat.

"You should get yourself a beer at the pub and try not to stress yourself out!" Reid calls, the current lazily taking him away as he avoids thinking about how much power paddling he'll be stuck doing to get back.

The sun overhead is hot and unforgiving. He mentally pats himself on the back for making sure to smother himself in sunscreen, and silently thanks the trees on either side of the river for providing at least a little shade. Despite the beauty and calm of nature around him, his heart pounds as he paddles to where he remembers seeing her first. The Town of Lake Tulrid isn't known for much. Located in the middle of fuck-nowhere-Canada, the small community doesn't see too many tourists apart from the occasional couple looking to escape city life for some country fun during those hot summer months, and those that come visiting never stick around for long. There isn't much in terms of accommodations other than a bed and breakfast that closes during the winter months, and a Flying J truck stop where you can grab a shower and a coffee if you happen to be passing through in the middle of the night. If you're looking to kill time at the local shops, the Town of Lake Tulrid is especially disappointing. There is a combination pharmacy and grocery store, a big-name hardware store, two competing gas stations, a Salvation Army, and a store that exclusively sells hunting goods. If you want a warm meal but don't want to cook, you can either enjoy some food at the pub, grab baked goods at the coffee shop, or drive to the pizza place an hour out of town.

He can't blame the tourists that up and left in the middle of the night, or went on nature hikes and didn't bother coming back. For most of his life, Reid has wished that for himself. With lumber and forestry being the main trades of the town, Reid had spent the bulk of his teen years dreading the day when he'd graduate and find himself working alongside his father in the lumber yard. Thankfully his parents had saved enough money to send him away to university, and when he'd come back from his studies he had quickly found himself a job teaching at his former school. The previous gym teacher had seemingly left town the month before and had never bothered to come back.

A bird calls out overhead, and two more answer back. He smiles at the summer sky, trying to relax as the lake gets nearer.

He hates lying, especially to his best friend, but the truth... well, the truth wouldn't make sense. How could he tell his friend he wants to visit the statue?

No, not wants. *Needs.*

There's a statue in the middle of Lake Tulrid, and no one's quite sure how it got there. It's a mermaid sculpted out of copper that never seems to tarnish. Her hair hangs in waves over her shoulders and down her back, her sharp features look out into the water in contemplation, and her scales glisten like opals in the sun as her tail wraps around the pillar she sits on. Each year the water of Lake Tulrid gets higher, but somehow she always stays above the ever-rising blue.

He'd seen her before on his other trips out to the water and hadn't thought much of her. But a few weeks ago, he'd been on the water with two tourists he'd befriended from St. James, and they'd been mesmerized by the way her figure caught the light. The longer he'd stared at her, the more human she'd looked. Her metal skin had seemed to soften and glow, singing out to him until he'd wanted to reach out and touch it for himself.

And he almost had, but the kayakers had wanted to make it back to town before the pub stopped serving dinner and, not one to leave a traveller behind, Reid had led them back to shore. Unfortunately, they hadn't shared his idealistic view of friendship, and were gone the next day without ever saying goodbye.

The statue had haunted his thoughts, calling to him ever since. His old car had broken down and he'd yet to replace it, so when Thomas had said that he needed to take the truck into town for an oil change, he'd jumped at the opportunity to revisit the mermaid of Lake Tulrid before school started in a few days.

He rounds a bend and then another, paddling faster as the water begins to slow and the neck of the river begins to widen. He holds his breath as he passes the last thicket of trees and... there she is.

The statue is exactly as he remembers it. The image of perfection moulded in copper. He paddles forwards, letting the water carry him the last of the way to the base of her seat. Her tail is long and muscular, and he notices both her teeth and nails are sharpened to a point. He stares up at her, and slowly, ever so slowly, the light begins to work its magic on her body.

The dark metal begins to soften, her skin deepening to olive. The strands of her hair loosen and relax, a weight lifting from them, the burnished metal darkening to locks of midnight. He watches as the scales on her body wake up, one by one, and blossom into a kaleido-scopic pattern of shimmering azure and seaweed green that moves and sways with the wind. Her eyes, as black as her hair, stare fixed at the lake as she ignores Reid.

"You look so real," he tells the statue.

He positions his kayak against the rocks of the statue and uses the paddle to keep the boat flush with the mermaid as he steps out onto the base of her short pillar. He grabs the edge and hoists himself onto the pillar. He nearly falls off, the copper slick from the water, but manages to hold on. His paddle, on the other hand, slips from his hand and lands in the boat, which lazily floats a few feet away from his spot. But Reid doesn't mind.

He marvels at the craftsmanship of the mermaid, the details etched into her body with care and precision. But it's the way her skin shines in the light, entrancing him, that he can't get enough of. It sparkles and dances, singing to be touched.

And so he does.

Reid reaches out a hand and runs it down the mermaid's arm, staring as it leaves a trail of goosebumps in his wake and feeling her flesh move under his fingertips. He looks up at her face and sees her eyes looking back at him. Before he can move, she reaches out a hand of her own and strokes the side of his face.

He grins as warmth spreads through his body. His legs stiffen and grow heavy, his ribs tightening and refusing to draw breath, his smile frozen in perpetuity. The mermaid leans forward and pushes Reid off the side of her pillar. As he falls back into the water, he uses the last of his energy to throw his hands out towards her, staring up into her face as she watches him sink into the lake.

No, he thinks as he descends past a hundred strange faces, *don't leave me down here. I want to see you. I want to be with you! Please, I love you!*

He drifts into the deep, joining the heap of men piled onto one another with arms thrown up in desperate adoration. Around him are men he's met but never got the chance to know: the kayakers he'd thought had left town and the former gym teacher. But he doesn't care about them, he cares about *her*.

As his heart finally turns to stone and his mind begins to quiet, he watches as the light hits her gleaming copper skin. She sits, triumphant, on her pillar, lifting herself higher as she stays above the ever-rising blue.

BARMBRACK

She stands at the back of the room, staring into the mirror suspended above her dresser. The candle flickers, shadows dancing around her. She gazes into the blackness of the reflection, eyes straining from the effort as she watches the darkened spot just behind her shoulder, and waits impatiently for the man to reveal himself.

"Are you coming down soon, sweetie?" her mother calls up. "Your colcannon's going to get cold."

She keeps her focus on the mirror, holding her breath in anticipation.

"Rileigh?" Holly asks again.

She exhales sharply, frustrated, blowing out the candle. "Yes, coming!"

She gives the mirror one last stare before turning away, crossing the small bedroom, and opening the door. Light from her parents' room brightens the hallway, and a buttery smell wafting up from the kitchen greets her at the top of the stairs. She can already feel the frustration melting away, her desire for food replacing her desire for answers, as she descends to the ground floor. Each step groans and complains beneath her, the floors having been redone before she was born and the house having been built long before that.

"Rileigh, can you help set the table?" Cael asks from the stove. They hold the massive pot of colcannon firmly with one hand, stirring wildly with a thick wooden spoon held in the other. Beside them, Rileigh's mom covers a tray with plastic wrap.

"Sure thing, Moddy!"

She gathers up some placemats from under the kitchen counter, grabs a handful of napkins, and scoops up some utensils from a drawer. She dresses the table in the adjacent room before going back to pick up a pitcher of water from the fridge and some drinking glasses.

"Alright everyone, I expect butts in chairs and healthy appetites," her mom says, carrying out two plates of food. "That means you too, Emma!"

Footsteps come racing up from the basement, the door exploding open and nearly knocking the other parent—arms full with dishes— over.

"Easy does it," they say with a smile.

"Sorry, Moddy!" the little girl says with enthusiasm, wrapping her arms around their waist and giving them a tight hug. She jumps on her chair at the table and beams at Rileigh. "Look," she says excitedly, "it fits!"

Her older sister smiles at her. "That's good! You can't go trick-or-treating as a witch without the right hat."

"Or spells!"

"Right, or spells. Otherwise, how will you get extra candy or turn bullies into toads?"

Rileigh picks up her fork and uses it to shovel a heap of the colcannon into her mouth. It's not the fanciest meal, but the warm cabbage and potato blend has always been one of her favourites, although she's not sure if that's because of the taste or because it's a Halloween specialty.

"So, what were you doing upstairs?" Cael asks between bites.

"Nothing."

"Which means something," her moddy deciphers.

"Rileigh told me she was going to look for a husband," Emma offers helpfully, a glob of potato threatening to fall off her fork and onto the table.

"You were what now?" her mom asks, confused.

"I was just curious if, you know, I'd see him this year."

"It's 'cause she likes Corey," Emma says happily, "and wants him to like her back."

"Emma, can you shut the hell up?" Rileigh yells, her face turning maroon with embarrassment. She doesn't just like Corey, she's pretty sure she loves him... even if she hasn't technically spoken to him yet. With him being two grades older than her, just the idea of speaking to him puts her in a cold sweat.

"Language," the two parents say in unison.

"What? You do!"

"Rileigh, can you explain to us what you were doing?" Holly insists.

"It was just that stupid candle thing. Grandma told me a while ago that she saw grandpa on Halloween in her mirror. She said if I wanted to see who I was going to marry one day, that I needed to light a candle in a dark room and look into a mirror on Halloween. It didn't work though."

"Because life is unpredictable, sweetie. If it was that easy to figure out who you're going to marry, your moddy and I could have saved ourselves a lot of time."

"I'm surprised nan would encourage you to do that though. I'll have to have a word with her the next time she calls," Cael says.

Rileigh nods, but keeps her doubt to herself. Scrying in the mirror may not have worked, but that doesn't mean everything else will fail too. She hopes her parents forget to confront her grandmother the next time she phones for a chat, since she'd also provided her with the other rituals Rileigh has planned for tonight. In truth, her grandmother had told her about some of the ways she and her sisters had celebrated the holiday growing up, and the ideas had gotten Rileigh thinking.

Soon the conversation turns to the evening's activities in Alexandria, the small town that neighbours their hobby farm. Surrounded by wheat fields, forests, dairy farms, and small-scale hatcheries, the community makes an effort to help facilitate trick-or-treating for local farming families. With the distance between rural properties so vast that most kids could walk all night and only get four candy bars, most shops stay open late to hand out chocolate and sweets, while the town holds a huge bonfire in the church parking lot. Most years, the smoke is so thick and so high that people miles away can still see it in the starry night sky from their homes.

"Who's ready for a slice of barmbrack?" their moddy asks eagerly.

"I am!" Emma screams, jumping to her feet and running with her late into the kitchen as Cael follows closely behind. Rileigh waits with her mom at the table, her heart beating nervously, as the two come back with the cling-wrapped tray.

"Remember," Holly says as Emma takes a seat and Cael sets the tray down, "each slice has a prize, so be careful when you eat your piece. I don't want anyone chipping a tooth."

Emma chooses her slice the second the plastic is removed. Rileigh is slower, more meticulous, carefully evaluating each slice before deciding on one. Her parents each grab a slice and, on the count of three, everyone tears into the fruitcake-like dessert. Emma almost immediately spits out a ring onto her plate, and her sister is suddenly furious. She wanted the ring, and the promise of a wedding that it brings. She huffs, annoyed, and keeps her fingers crossed that her slice at least holds the coin in it, promising wealth. She takes another bite, this time finding the small metal prize with her teeth, and spits it out into her napkin.

It's a thimble. Her heart sinks.

"This is bullshit!" she shouts, eyes filling with tears.

"Language!" her mom shouts back.

"It's not fair! Emma gets the ring, and I get the thimble? She's going to marry first and I'm not going to marry at all? I'm the older sister, I should get the ring. It's not fair!"

She knows she's acting childish. She knows it's just a game. She can feel herself spinning out of control, like a toddler having a tantrum in the middle of a store, but she can't seem to stop herself no matter how much she wants to. She's sobbing now, gasping for air between heaves.

"Rileigh, calm down," her mom says gently, rubbing her upper back, "it's just for fun, sweetie. The prizes are just part of the game, they don't mean anything seriously. I got the thimble the year I met your moddy, and the coin the year I lost my office job. It's not the outcome of this game that matters, but what you make of the year between now and next Halloween."

"I just really want him to like me," she snivels.

Her mom picks up the thimble, cleaning it of food and placing it in Rileigh's hand.

"It's normal to get crushes at your age, sweetie. But if he doesn't feel the same way about you, that's okay! It just means someone better suited for you is out there."

She wants to argue and shout and tell them it's more than a crush, it's love. It's true love. Instead, she nods in agreement and puts the thimble in her pocket, finishing her barmbrack in silence between shaky breaths.

"Alright everyone, get your plates in the kitchen, get into your costumes, and we'll head out soon. Sound good?" Cael says cheerfully.

Emma agrees enthusiastically and runs back down to the basement without cleaning up after herself. Rileigh brings her dish in with Emma's and then heads upstairs to get ready. She's not going trick-or-treating this year, but instead will be meeting her friend at the bonfire.

"Rileigh," her mom calls as she heads upstairs, "remember to take your asthma inhaler before we go."

"Sure thing!"

She opens the door to the medicine cabinet in the upstairs bathroom. Her small turbuhaler sits on the shelf next to the deep green bottle of melatonin.

Melatonin!

"Yes!" she hisses under her breath. It's exactly what she needs, and a renewed sense of excitement grows inside her. She takes the supplement from the cabinet and pours a few pills into the palm of her hand. The last time she took the sleep aid, it did nothing but make her feel sluggish—albeit awake—throughout the night. This time, knowing her final ritual depends on her being asleep, she's determined to make the pills work. She slips five of them under her tongue, following the instructions and letting them dissolve completely, before returning the bottle to the cabinet.

In her bedroom, she turns on the light and picks up her backpack off the floor. Inside are two small baggies. The first holds a handful of hazelnuts and is the reason she needs to go to the bonfire tonight. The second bag contains sugared walnuts, a few honeyed hazelnuts, and a dash of nutmeg. She opens this bag and eats the sweet concoction, swallowing the final notes of the chalky pills with it.

Her grandmother hadn't been specific about how much of the nut medley she would have to eat in order to get visions of her future husband. She had, however, been adamant that Rileigh needed to be asleep in order to have the prophetic dreams. Between how high her emotions have been all day, and what she's sure will be a lot of excitement in town, she hopes the melatonin will be able to guarantee her at least a few minutes of dream-filled rest. With any luck, her timing will work out perfectly, and she will be in the car on the way home when the pills start to kick in. Otherwise, her family's quick trip into town is about to become an exceptionally long one.

She throws the remaining bag of nuts into her purse along with her wallet and some lip gloss—just in case Corey's there—before giving her hair a quick brush. She feels the thimble from her slice of cake in her pocket, and throws it into her purse too for good measure. Her moddy calls up to her and, feeling hopeful about things to come, she hurries back downstairs.

———

ALTHOUGH THE DRIVE into Alexandria isn't longer than usual, it feels that way to the sisters. Emma is practically jumping out of her skin with excitement at the prospect of collecting a pillowcase's worth of candy, while Rileigh's imagination runs wild with scenarios in which she accidentally-on-purpose runs into Corey. When they park the car at the public library, it takes both girls visible restraint not to rip off their seatbelts and bolt out of the car.

"Rileigh, I want you to meet us back here, at the car, by nine. Not nine-oh-one, not nine-fifteen, nine on the dot."

"Yes, Mom."

"I don't care if you run into all your friends, if you run into a squad of cute boys, or if you're running late for any reason. You make it back here for nine or you're grounded, got it kiddo?"

"I know, I know."

"You say that, but then you're always late."

"Tonight will be different."

"It better be," she says before giving her a big hug. "If you need us for any reason, call your moddy. I forgot my cell at home, but they've got theirs, okay?"

"Sounds good!"

She waves to her parents and heads off towards the church before they can add any more instructions or caveats to the list. It isn't a long walk from the library to her destination—nothing in Alexandria is much of a far walk away from anything else. She suspects that if her sister had successfully convinced her parents to take them to Cornwall this year, like she almost had, she wouldn't have been granted nearly as much liberty with her time this evening. It's the first year she's been allowed to spend Halloween without them, finally having convinced her parents and Emma that she's too adult to go trick-or-treating. And while she's excited to spend the night with her friend Darcy, she's even more excited to test her luck—and her grandmother's last ritual for finding her future husband—at the bonfire.

"Ri, over here!" Darcy is leaning against a no-parking sign and waves cheerfully. Her jean jacket is tied around her waist, the air thick with heat from the fire on an otherwise chilly night.

At the far end of the parking lot is the enormous bonfire. Huge clouds of thick grey smoke rise up into the black sky. Even though she's not directly in the path of the smoke, Rileigh's throat already feels tight from the heaviness of it. The back of her mouth tastes ashy, and she realizes with some annoyance that she never did grab her inhaler.

"Hey! How's it been so far?" she asks, giving her friend a hug.

"It's been fine, I guess. Like, they haven't really done much. They've just been chucking wood on the fire," she says, gesturing to a lumber pile of fir and red cedar. "Everyone claps when the smoke gets bigger or the flames get taller and whatever."

Rileigh's eyes scan the crowd and she lets out a long yawn. "Do you know if Corey's here?"

"Nah, he probably wouldn't be caught dead at something this lame, you know?"

She deflates a little. "Yeah, totally."

"Did you want to go check out the shops? I think a few of the second-hand ones are open still, like, for business. My mom gave me allowance so we could totally go do some thrifting and snag some free candy too. Wanna go?"

"Yeah, sure. I just want to get a little closer to the bonfire first."

"Oh, are you still doing that weird thing with the nuts?"

"It's not weird," she says defensively, "it's old-school. And it won't take long, either."

"What are you doing again?"

"I'm going to give one of the hazelnuts the name of my crush and then throw them all on the fire. If his nut turns to ash, he's my true love."

"And if it doesn't?"

"It will."

"But if it doesn't?"

"Then I don't want to talk about it."

"How are you going to get close though?"

"Whadamean?" she asks through a yawn.

"Uh, what?"

"Sorry," Rileigh says shaking her head from side to side. "I'm sleepy tonight. I said, 'what do you mean?'"

"The police are keeping people back from the fire. See?" Darcy nods to an officer a few meters in front of the blaze.

"Ummm, okay. Well, can you distract him?"

"Are you serious?"

"Darcy, you owe me one."

"I don't know. My mom would be really mad if she found out. And like, what if I get in trouble with the cops? I don't know if that's really worth going to juvie for."

Rileigh rolls her eyes dramatically, before coughing into the crook of her elbow. "You're not going to go to juvie, idiot. You can just tell him you lost your phone or something and he'll have to help you find it. I'll sneak around super quick and be back before he notices I'm there." When Darcy hesitates, Rileigh clasps her hands in front of her heart and pouts her bottom lip out. "Pleeeeaaaaase."

"Fiiiine. But you're letting me copy off your math homework for the rest of next week."

"Yeah, yeah, deal."

The two girls make their way forward in the small crowd that's gathered near the fire. Rileigh makes sure to put some distance between herself and her friend, doing her best to get on the left side of the officer, while Darcy approaches him from the right. She watches as Darcy asks him for help, doing her best to seem upset but mostly coming across as nervous. The second the cop's attention is on her, Rileigh moves as fast as her now-tired legs can move. She circles around to the back of the fire, making sure to put the wall of flames between her and the eyes of the spectators, and crosses her fingers that nobody tells the officer she's gotten closer.

Her eyes water as the smoke hits her like a wall. Her lungs feel hotter than the fire, and she coughs hard. She grabs the bag of hazelnuts from her purse and rushes to get it open, fingers fumbling along the seam. With a surprising amount of effort, she fumbles the bag open, its contents spilling onto the ground around the fire.

"No!"

Rileigh drops to her hands and knees, trying to pick up the small brown spheres to throw them in the flames as they roll away on the hard pavement. The smoke surrounds her face, billowing up around her in a heavy grey cloud. She coughs again and inhales deeply, trying to catch her breath, but the hot ashy air pushes its way deeper into her lungs. She can feel her lungs seizing and struggling, each breath burning deep within her chest, her nostrils and mouth searing from the smoke.

Her hands feel heavy and each finger feels too big as she tries to fish her cell phone out from her purse. She coughs, chest heaving from the effort of expelling the hot air, and struggles to wrap her fingers around the device. Her body feels like it's moving through water, each movement taking longer than it should, each action exhausting. She presses her thumb to the home button and the phone unlocks with a click before slipping through her limp fingers and falling to the ground.

She struggles to pull in air, each inhalation only welcoming more smoke.

Her arms eventually give out, pins and needles dancing under her skin, as she crashes onto her side, the contents of her purse spilling out around her. She wheezes, the heat from the fire burning her skin, her eyelids heavy.

The last thing she sees before her eyes finally close is the glint of the silver thimble winking in the flames.

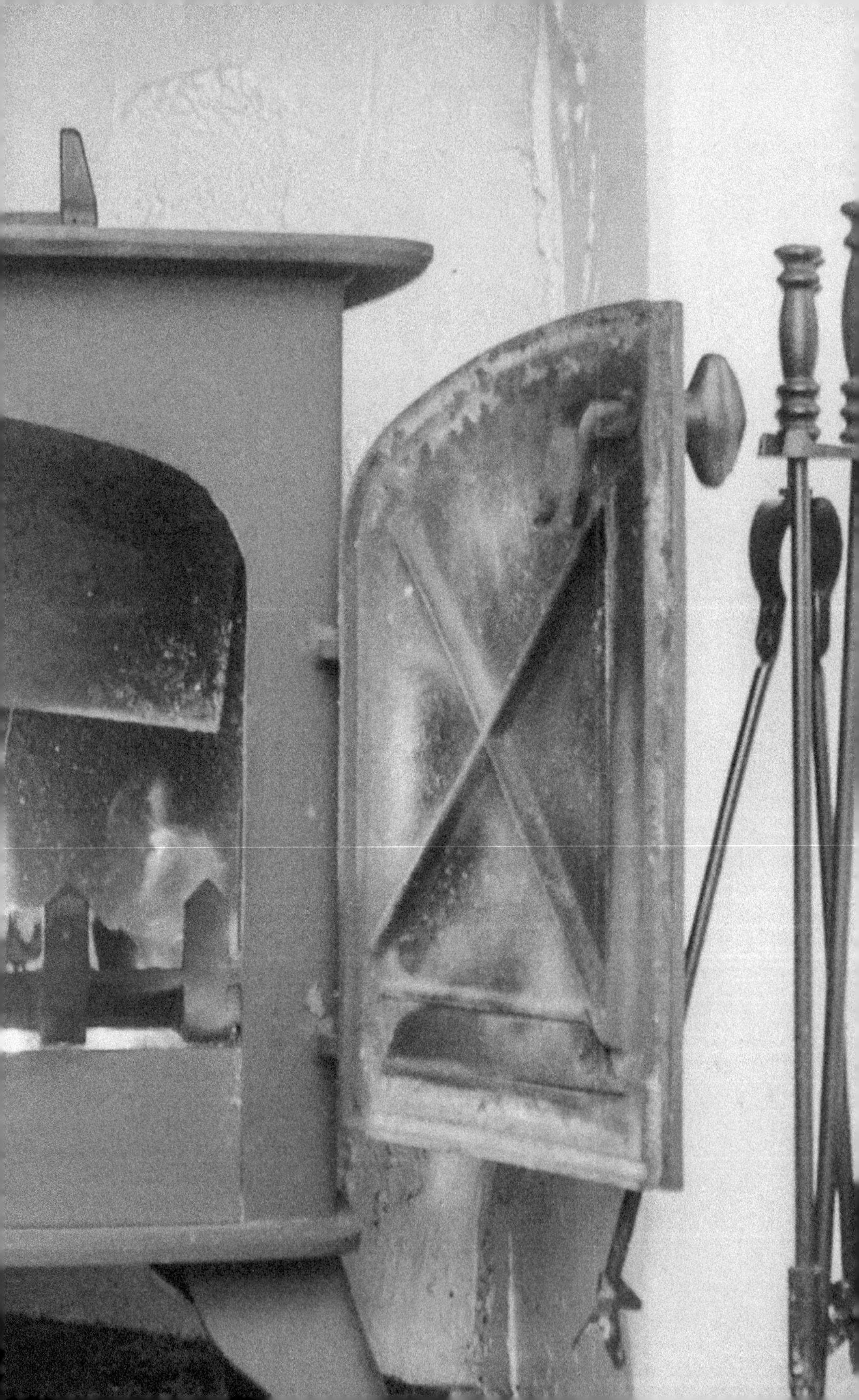

———

DOIREANN

———

SHE OPENS THE FRONT DOOR AND STEPS INTO THE TINY SPACE, THE harsh winds and stiff hinge slamming the door closed behind her. The mudroom shakes from the force of the slam as she hangs up her jacket on an old metal hook and rests her heavy boots on one of the cheap plastic mats. She crosses the space, accidentally stepping in a newly-formed puddle of melted snow, and opens the slightly less rickety door to the living room. A blast of warm air greets her as she enters, and only once she's beside the fireplace does she peel off her wet socks.

Doireann watches her granddaughter from where she sits on the old rocking chair, knuckles turning white as she tightens her grip on the wooden knitting needles.

"Is it true?"

Shona doesn't say anything, instead choosing to rub her hands together near the open flames. Doireann takes this as an answer.

"How is Art taking it?"

"He doesn't know. Nobody's told him yet."

"Why not?" she says angrily, pulling the yarn taut behind one of the needles.

"Because he's sick too, *mamó*. They don't expect he'll make it through the night."

"Is that what the doctor told you?"

"No, he wasn't there. Fiona told me that he's not even able to make it out of Hopedale, let alone make the trek north, since the town is as badly snowed in as we are. She's not even sure when the coroner will be able to come get her mum. He couldn't promise anything when she rang him up, and when she tried again the line was down. It's amazing she was even able to phone out the first time."

Doireann nods solemnly. She's known Nora all her life. Both had come from Irish immigrant families, both had been too poor to finish school, and both had even done something their own parents had failed to do: grow old.

"Has Aileen been over to begin keening while she tends to her father?"

"She doesn't want any of that, especially with him still alive in the house."

"She's waiting until after, then?"

Shona shakes her head, finally looking away from the fire to meet her mother's gaze.

"I don't think she wants it at all. Too depressing."

Doireann shakes her head, purses her lips, and begins to rock in the old chair. She finishes her row of stitches with the thick white yarn before setting it down in her lap.

"When will the wake start?"

"I don't think there will be one. Not with the weather as it is and Art so sick."

"Not even afterwards?"

"No."

"Not even for him?"

Shona shakes her head. "Not even for him."

"There won't even be a proper burial with the way she's going on like this."

"She's having them cremated."

"Cremated!" Doireann chokes. "That's not right. That's just not right. That's not how we do it. That's not how we show the dead respect."

Shona huffs as she gets to her feet. Her hair glows as red as the flames as she stands in their light, looking sadly at the old woman.

"It's how she's doing it, *mamó*. It's how she's respecting her parents, or hopefully just her mum, God willing."

"It's not what Nora would have wanted."

"You can't know that for sure. Besides, this is what Fiona wants; to grieve alone and to grieve in quiet, to hold onto the ashes of her mother, and to keep on trying to live." Even though she doesn't add more, Doireann knows the unspoken truth Shona refuses to give voice to: it's what she would have wanted for her mother. She hated the group of keening women gathered around her mother's body, the days-long wake, the blazing church in the summer heat, the procession of her mother's coffin through the town to the graveyard. It was a funeral rite Doireann always thought she would have for herself one day, not give to her child.

Shona leans down and kisses her grandmother on the forehead, her chapped lips rough on Doireann's wrinkled and delicate skin. "I'll get dinner on."

Doireann picks her knitting back up, trying not to wallow in sadness as she continues to expertly work the bulky yarn. She used to pity herself for losing her parents so young in life, but now she wonders if them dying young was really a form of kindness. At least they didn't have to watch as their language, traditions, and stories were forgotten by the generations after them, the very people who had sworn to protect what was left after the English had already stomped so much of it out.

Shona comes back with the cast iron pot and suspends it over the fire. She stirs the contents with a ladle and then takes a seat on the floor again.

"There wasn't much left in the kitchen," she admits sadly. "I used the bones from the chicken leg we split the other night, some of the soft pine that Ros cut for us, and the last quarter of the turnip we had. Once the pine is done... I'm not sure what we'll do."

"Take the chicken bones out before it's done stewing, and we can use them again in another broth, *aingeal*."

"What does that mean again?"

"Sweetie," Doireann says, trying to keep the disappointment out of her voice. She'd failed to teach her daughter much Irish, and had failed even worse with her granddaughter. "And Turlough's passing by with some salted venison tomorrow in exchange for these wool socks, if the roads stay open long enough for him to make his way out here."

"That's a big 'if,' *mamó*. It's bad out there. I'd be shocked if the radio didn't warn of a whiteout tonight, or if the radio didn't cut out in our sleep. I just hope the telephone lines are still up come morning so we can check on how Art is doing."

Doireann knows Shona really means to check if Art is still alive.

Doireann also knows he won't be.

First spring flooding and then a summer drought; the crops hadn't stood a chance. It wasn't long until the town was facing the same food shortage as the rest of the province, along with the exceedingly harsh winter. Empty bellies led to weak constitutions, and what had once been a strong community of elders was soon only a handful left once pneumonia had caught in town. Now, with Nora gone and Art not far behind, Doireann is practically the last *seanóir*. And if she has already failed to teach her granddaughter their language, their myths, and to respect their traditions, she doesn't see how she alone can keep the knowledge from her family's homeland alive.

Shona stirs the soup, making sure to set the chicken bones aside for another meal, before dishing herself and Doireann a bowl.

The two women eat in silence, neither full when the meal's over.

———

TURLOUGH DOESN'T COME the next day or the day after that, although news of Art's passing does. Fiona confirms Doireann's worst fears—a traditional funeral won't be held for her friends—and the phone line cuts out as she's relaying the information that Eamon has also fallen ill. Before the winter's out, Doireann knows that she'll be dead with the rest of the *seanóir* community. If disease doesn't get her, the hunger will.

Her parents had taught her of the blight their families had faced in Ireland. The starvation, the madness, the hard decisions made in the name of survival. It was a story she'd shared with a Ukrainian woman in Hopedale, who was all too familiar with the tale. *Like a devil's winter*, she'd said as she recalled stories of communities torn apart by hunger and desperation, of pacts made with demonic forces, covenants made in flesh, and unnatural transformations. *But even after the snow leaves, the monster remains.*

It takes some convincing, but eventually Shona agrees to take her to Fiona's house to pay her respects to her friends.

"If Nora's own daughter won't perform the funeral rites for her parents, then I will."

"She doesn't want that, *mamó*."

"But Nora would, if not for herself then for her husband's soul."

"Fiona doesn't want—"

"She doesn't need to know. I'll be quiet, I'll grieve alone, but I'll grieve proper."

Her granddaughter refuses at first, saying a journey for someone her age through the snow would be suicide, but Doireann is determined to go with or without her help, and so Shona begrudgingly gives in.

She does her best to stay warm, layering a cotton undershirt with first a sweater that moths have eaten away at and then with a sturdier one, corduroys on top of long johns and held by a belt. Everything is too big on her, after having been forced to lose weight since the year of bad luck started, but Doireann makes do. She makes sure to tuck a handkerchief into her pocket, hoping it won't be needed for her tears. Her fur coat sits heavily on her small frame, and the winter boots she straps on feel as heavy as cinder blocks. Despite the cumbersome winter gear, Doireann proves determined to make the hike to Fiona's and is out the door of the mudroom before Shona is finished dressing.

Even though she's been seeing the snow pile up from her window, the reality of it only hits her now. The field is covered in snowdrifts, some taller than she is, and the path from her house to the road would be invisible if not for the tips of the fenceposts that are still visible. The white is so thick and high it reaches her hip, and the sun overhead —whose rays of heat should be a welcomed gift—only serves to make the landscape blazing. She squints as she surveys her property, dread washing over her as she imagines the flooding the town will face once winter thaws into spring.

Shona leads the way to Fiona's house, using a small spade to help move some of the snow for Doireann to travel a bit easier. It's slow going, the two needing frequent breaks on what would otherwise be a twenty-minute walk, their empty stomachs an added burden on the arduous journey. By the time the two women arrive at their destination, Doireann is drenched in sweat and the only things interrupting her wheezing are her coughing fits and growling belly.

"I knew you shouldn't have done this, *mamó*."

Doireann doesn't dignify this with a response, and instead knocks hard on the front door. It takes a few raps, but eventually a red-eyed Fiona answers, her somber expression giving way to one of surprise.

"Shona, Doireann, what are you doing here?"

"I came to pay my respects."

"But," she looks accusingly at Shona, "I told you I'm not having a wake."

"I know," Doireann says before her granddaughter can answer, "and I promise I won't stay long, but Nora was like a sister to me. She was there for me when I lost my parents, my daughter, even my husband. I just want to say my goodbyes one last time. Please," she adds for emphasis.

Doireann isn't sure if it's her plea that persuades her, or the sad sight the two women make in the snow, but Fiona consents to let them in.

"I'd offer you black tea or whisky," she says as they strip their winter gear off in her mudroom, "but those both ran out a while ago. I can boil some spruce if you'd like though."

Doireann gives a hard cough.

"Might help with your chest, ma'am."

"That would be appreciated, thanks," Shona says for the two of them. "I'll come help."

"Where can I find them?" Doireann asks.

"Upstairs, the door at the end of the hall."

Fiona and Shona make their way to the kitchen, talking quietly, as Doireann follows the directions to Art and Nora. It takes her a while to climb the stairs, her legs sore from the long walk and her hips not what they used to be, and when she gets to the door it takes her even longer to open it. She wanted to say her final goodbyes, to do her part to uphold this tradition for her friends when no one else will, but now the task feels impossible and fills her with dread. And, worse, she can't help but wonder, who will do this for her when she goes? Who will mourn and keen and remember, when everyone else alive has already forgotten?

She makes her way into the bedroom, quietly closing the door and locking it behind her. Art and Nora lie side-by-side, hands nearly touching. Neither looks like Doireann remembers. Both are sunken in and hollowed out by age and illness. Their empty eyes look up at her, sightless, but she still feels like she's being watched. Fiona has sprayed the room thick with perfumes, but even the heavy scent can't hide the fact that the coroner is taking too long to collect their bodies. If the smell didn't give it away, the small gathering of coffin flies does. If he doesn't arrive soon then Fiona will have to pay Turlough, or another man in town, to help move her parents outside to the woodshed.

Doireann takes a seat on the bed next to them, the worn mattress sinking with a creak. So much knowledge in this bed, she thinks. So many traditions, so many stories, so much culture in this bed. Most of it already gone forever, the rest soon to join. Her growling stomach punctuates the silence.

A devil's winter... even after the snow leaves, the monster remains.

The thought leaves so suddenly, she wonders if she really had it.

The idea's repulsive, monstrous, and yet tantalizing. To survive winter, to just outrun the season, would give her enough time to pass the knowledge on. It would, she hopes, be just long enough to teach Shona the most important things and maybe even instil in her the unshakeable importance of carrying these traditions on to her own children one day. She thinks Nora would understand.

She studies their face in the dim candlelight of the bedroom, looking for some sign of consent, before she slowly unbuttons Nora's blouse and tugs at the sleeve. She uncovers the top of Nora's arm, the skin like wrinkled white leather, and eyes the fleshy part. Her stomach churns as she leans forward and bites. The texture is wrong, like old and jellied meat, and the rancid taste of old copper makes her gag. It's harder to bite through than she expected, but goes down easier than she hoped once she manages to pull a piece away. *Like eating old steak*, she lies to herself. She's suddenly thankful that she chose Nora instead of Art, her best friend being dead long enough to prevent any blood. Still, cautious of leaving evidence, she takes her handkerchief out of her pocket, wipes her mouth, and folds it into a thick cotton rectangle which she covers the wound with. She silently prays that any stains the blood leaves will stay on the cloth and won't seep through to Nora's blouse.

There's a knock at the door, and Doireann nearly jumps out of her skin.

"*Mamó*, your spruce tea is ready." Shona turns the handle to the room, but finds it locked. "*Mamó*? Is everything alright?"

"Yes," she says, doing up the last of Nora's buttons. It takes her two tries to get off the bed, her knees having difficulty with the height of it, and shuffles to open the door.

"Why was it locked?"

"I don't know, it shouldn't have been," she lies, trying to sound as concerned as Shona. She grabs the cup of tea from her granddaughter and takes a deep sip, letting the warm taste wash away the fleshy tang of her friend. Her stomach growls and churns, and Doireann feels suddenly unwell. She takes hold of Shona's arm for balance.

"Are you sure you're okay, *mamó*?" she asks, taking the tea back and helping to guide the old woman through the hall and down the stairs.

"I think it's just been a shock, *aingeal*. I never thought I'd have to live through something like this since your mother passed. And now —" she coughs, the force of it doubling her over.

"Is she okay?" Fiona asks, concern lining the soft edges of her face.

Although Doireann tries to convince them that all is well, by the time she's finished dressing in the coat she's drenched in sweat and shaking uncontrollably. Neither of the women want her to make the trip home, but she knows she can't stay. Not after what she's done, and not while there's so much left to do.

The trip home feels immeasurably longer than the trip to Fiona's had taken. By the time they get in, it's late afternoon, and Doireann is sure she's going to be sick all over the mudroom. She kicks off her boots as fast as her stiff joints will let her, leaves her furs on the floor, and makes a beeline for her bed. The room is cold and her sweat-covered clothing feels like ice on her skin, but she doesn't have the energy to change into something warm, let alone start a fire. Thankfully, Shona gets one started in the living room, and piles blankets on Doireann in the hopes that they'll suffice until the heat makes its way to her.

Doireann wants to cry, and if it weren't for the shivers she probably would be. How could she believe in demons? In pacts with the Devil? How could she do that to her friend? To a woman who was her sister by nearly every definition? It was a desperate attempt to save the last bits of her parents, but she should have known it was just an old wives' tale. It was just another story, like the stories her mother used to tell her about the banshees and the Dullahan. She'd been given limited time, and she's wasted the last of it. She can only hope Shona will remember for her.

Her bones ache. They feel hot inside her flesh, like they're covered in fire ants that eat away at her from the inside. Her hands and feet feel like they're being stretched out and run through a taffy puller. Is this what Nora had felt? Her stomach roars. Was this pain the last thing Art had known? Her pale skin is white in the glow of the afternoon sun. She feels as hollowed out as her friends looked. She closes her eyes and waits to die.

She sits up in bed, surrounded by darkness. There's a soft glow from the living room, the shadows from the fire dancing along the walls. Doireann is tired—exhausted—but it's the smell that keeps her from falling back asleep. Thick, fatty, and sweet. Her stomach screams in excitement.

The venison!

She pulls herself onto her feet, legs unsteady beneath her, as she makes her way down the narrow hall. Turlough must have come while she was under. She hopes Shona gave him the wool socks, otherwise he won't be so quick to share his spoils with them next time.

She plods around the kitchen, but doesn't find any food. The cupboards are bare, with the exception of some pine strips and needles for tea, but the fatty smell remains trapped in her nose. She crosses the space into the living room to find Shona asleep in front of the fire.

Sweet Shona.

Thick, fatty, sweet smelling Shona.

Her stomach growls and she can't help her mouth watering. Drool runs through the gaps between her sharp teeth, spilling out over her thin lips, and dribbling onto her chest. Shona coughs in her sleep, a deep, throaty expulsion of air. It's the same cough she had, the same cough Nora had. It was the same cough her daughter had had all those years ago.

Shona won't make it through winter.

But her story will, along with so many others. Doireann licks her lips as her stomach calls out.

A devil's winter. Even after the snow leaves, I'll remain.

MAGNUM OPUS

JANUARY

"Congratulations!" Kim screams from the front steps of the townhouse, carrying a bottle of pink champagne in one hand and a box of cupcakes tied with glittery ribbon in the other. Her breath frames her face in tendrils of silver as the snow lazily falls onto the concrete around her.

"Thank yoooooou!" Charlotte screams back, wrapping her arms around her friend in a hug before letting go and beckoning the other woman inside.

Kim kicks her boots off onto the shoe rack by the door before stepping out of the entranceway and into the small home. Charlotte takes the pastries and alcohol, bringing them into the kitchen while Kim shrugs off her winter coat and tosses it carelessly onto one of the metal hooks on the wall.

"You must be excited," Kim says, taking a seat at the kitchen island as Charlotte rinses out a set of old champagne flutes. They were a wedding present from her mother that she'd only ever used once before: after signing her divorce papers.

"I am excited! But it's really not that big of a deal. I kind of feel silly celebrating, to be honest," she says, cheeks warm and coloured pink.

"Why would you be embarrassed?"

"I don't know. I just, I guess it's not that big of a deal and we're treating it like one," she lies.

It *is* a big deal and she *is* excited, but she doesn't want to admit this to Kim.

"It's a *huge* deal," Kim argues. "You have a book coming out from a major publisher! What's not to get excited about?"

"I don't know. I mean, it's not like it's my first one. And, let's be honest, it's not like it's going to be as big as yours have been."

Kim waves a hand dismissively. "It's going to be bigger. I can feel it. Besides, it's not like publishing's a competition anyway, right?"

"Right!"

Wrong. It isn't a competition for Kim because she's already won.

Kim Lavoie. *The* Kim Lavoie, a household name when it comes to all things romantic comedy. Her books have made the New York Times Best Seller List, are frequently raved about by middle-aged housewives stuck in monogamous vanilla marriages, and are even in the process of being adapted into a TV series by Netflix (although Kim refuses to confirm the details with anyone, even Charlotte). She writes quirky romances about the joys of domesticity, uplifting stories that could never come true. Despite her background in literature, having studied it in university alongside Charlotte, her writing is designed with entertainment—not literary canon—in mind.

Kim is, to put it bluntly, everything Charlotte dislikes about popular writers today. Not that she'll ever admit that to her friend.

"Do you want any help?"

"No, I've got it," Charlotte says, drying the flutes with a dish towel and setting them down on the island next to the champagne. She takes out two small plates and a stack of napkins and sets them down next to the cupcakes, a smile plastered on her face as she moves about the room. With a pair of scissors, she cuts through the metallic ribbon and opens the white bakery box.

"Don't they look good?" Kim asks.

"Amazing," Charlotte says, emphasizing the second syllable of the word and feeling like a sorority girl in the process. "*So* classy looking."

"Right? Totally swanky," Kim laughs, taking one out of the box. It's decorated with millennial pink frosting with white sprinkles, perfectly matching the champagne.

Charlotte grabs one with white swirls of frosting and a dusting of edible silver. She bites into it, revealing a funfetti cake with a strawberry compote centre.

"Delicious," Charlotte says, mouth full. Kim nods enthusiastically.

"Want me to pop it?" She gestures at the bottle.

"I've got it," Charlotte tells her, twisting off the metal cage covering the top. She places both thumbs under the lip of the cork and pushes upward, turns the bottle, repositions her thumbs, and presses upward again. She repeats the process a few times before the cork dislodges with a loud pop. She pours the alcohol into the crystal glasses, and the two women clink them together in cheers before taking a sip of bubbly pink liquid.

"So, what's the book called?"

"*And All the Rivers Burned*," Charlotte says proudly.

"Ooh! So dramatic! I love it! And what's it about? I mean, if I can ask?" Kim says, resting her chin on her hand as she leans against the wooden top of the island.

"It's a story about death and divorce. This woman and her husband have lost their son to leukaemia and his death drives them apart. So, we see the woman try to navigate both of these losses while discovering herself."

"That sounds amazing... and really heavy. I can't wait to cry my eyes out while I read it."

"Yeah, it's definitely intense," Charlotte admits. "But I really think it's my best book yet. Like, I don't know how to explain it, but it just *feels* like art is supposed to feel. You know?"

"Definitely," Kim says with a smile.

Charlotte grins back at her, trying hard to quiet the envious voice in the back of her brain that doubts the other woman knows what great art is, let alone that she's ever written any. She tries to ignore the part of herself that belittles Kim's books and reduces them to just cheesy romances that capitalize on sex, scandal, and cheap tropes. It's hard to do; Charlotte likes to think her own work has always been *real* art that focuses on what really matters. It examines loss, identity, and womanhood. The things that define us. The things that are important.

Even if those things don't sell quite as many books. Charlotte takes another sip of her drink.

"And it comes out in April, right?" Kim asks.

"Yeah."

"Oh, this is going to be so exciting! I was really hoping we'd have books out at the same time again."

Charlotte suddenly feels like she's free-falling, as though the floor has opened up beneath her.

"What?"

"Well," Kim says sheepishly, "that's part of what I came here to celebrate. They moved the release date of my next book to April, right in time for Mother's Day! Although I'm not really sure *why* they're moving it; this isn't a romance like my other books. It's more of a murder mystery with elements of—"

"Your book is coming out in April too," Charlotte interrupts, throat tight. It's not a question.

"Yeah! Our books are going to be coming out at the same time!"

"Yay!" Charlotte forces out before draining the rest of her drink.

Her heart thunders furiously against her rib cage. She already knows what will happen in a few months: Kim's book will outsell hers. Any praise, any sales, any notoriety she was hoping to get from this new book is dead in the water. Her book will be forgotten and left unread on shelves, or worse, will be doomed to gather dust at the bottom of discount book bins.

Just like the last time.

"I knew you'd be excited!" Kim enthuses. "Of course I am! Why wouldn't I be?"

Kim shrugs. "I know book releases can be a really personal thing and I didn't want to step on your toes, you know? But like, the books are so different that I can't see it being a problem."

"Obviously," Charlotte grits out. She grabs the bottle of pink champagne and pours more into her own flute before refilling Kim's as well.

She lifts her glass, Kim mirroring her, and tilts it back and downs the whole thing. She pours another round from the bottle, Kim shaking her head as her glass is filled to the top.

"Oh, I shouldn't. I'm driving and I'm a *total* lightweight."

"It's just one more drink. I'm sure you'll be fine."

Kim hesitates before lifting the glass to her lips. Charlotte knows she shouldn't pressure her friend to drink, especially when Kim has always had a hard time controlling herself around liquor, but she doesn't care. She's too upset to think clearly.

She downs her own drink again.

"You must really like that champagne," Kim laughs before swallowing hers back too.

"Well, it's a night to celebrate, isn't it? We *both* have books coming out this year, after all. If that isn't a reason to celebrate, I don't know what is."

The plastic smile falls off her face as she turns away from Kim and walks through the doorway to the living room. She grabs a few bottles of heavy liquor from the bar cart and returns to the tiny kitchen to mix some drinks. Kim squirms excitedly in her seat when she sees the tequila, tapping on her cellphone's screen to check the time.

"I guess it's time to party!" Kim yells, clapping her hands with excitement.

"Totally."

———

BY THE TIME Kim gets up from her seat at the table, she's had more drinks than either of them can count. What started off as a few glasses of champagne quickly turned into shots, a couple of mixed drinks, and an entire bottle of wine. Now, Charlotte watches as Kim holds onto the back of a wooden chair for dear life, her legs shaking as she struggles to stand on her own.

Across the table from her, Charlotte messily eats her third cupcake, the buzz from the booze already starting to wear while the depression sets in even harder. She licks the frosting off the top and nibbles at the bottom of the pastry, not noticing—or not caring—

that the cream filling is leaking from one of the holes she's made in the base of the cake. She chews with her mouth open and takes small sips of her water, trying to dull the hangover she's already getting.

"Y-you still have wine," Kim says, speech slurred and sluggish as she points. The glass of red rests on the table next to Charlotte, the wine leaving streaks down the thin glass and forming rings on the hard-wood table. Charlotte can't begin to worry right now about how she's going to try (and fail) to clean them off.

"Yup," she says, voice gravelly from the alcohol.

Kim flaps her hand, pantomiming for her friend to pass over the rest of the wine. Charlotte rolls her eyes and slides the glass over, her stomach churning as she watches the red liquid slosh against the walls of the glass. Although Kim is finally standing, Charlotte suspects she doesn't actually have the coordination to move anywhere given her level of intoxication. Although Charlotte stopped drinking a few hours ago, the liquor having only numbed her face and not her fury, she's been popping Tylenol and Tums like candy in an attempt to stop the already developing headache and nausea.

Kim picks up the glass and throws the drink back in a single gulp as Charlotte watches, revolted.

"How the fuck are you still going?"

"Huh?" Kim asks, eyes unfocused as she sets the empty stemware down and looks at her friend.

"Never mind."

"What? W-what'd you say?"

"Nothing, Kim. You should sit down. You're going to fall."

"B-ut you'll catch me!" she slurs happily. Her cheeks are rosy and she grins wide like a child, her teeth tinted red from the wine.

"No. You'll fall, hit my floor, and crack your head open. Sit the fuck down," Charlotte tells her flatly.

Kim frowns and looks down at the ground sadly, only half aware of how rudely she's being talked to. Charlotte feels a twinge of guilt at how she's treating her friend, but she's more ashamed that part of her enjoys how cruel she's being. She knows it's not Kim's fault that her book's release was moved up, and she knows that her friend only has the best of intentions, but it doesn't stop her from hating the situation or from hating herself for how jealous she is of Kim.

She adds, "Please, I really don't want to clean blood off of hardwood."

"You're fun-ny," Kim laughs, letting go of the wooden chair and trying her luck at standing on her own. Her legs shake and her body wobbles with each small step that she takes. She makes for the sofa, her eyes struggling to stay open. Charlotte is tempted to stick a leg out as Kim passes her by, but she stops herself, sick with shame that the thought of hurting her friend had even crossed her mind.

"Here," Charlotte huffs, pushing herself up from the table and wrapping an arm around Kim's waist, the awful feeling spurring her into a selfish act of kindness. Although she's not quite as steady on her feet as she'd like to be, she's able to help support Kim's weight as she stumbles into the other room.

"Th-ah-n-kss," Kim mumbles.

Kim's head lolls onto her chest and her feet drag on the ground as Charlotte practically carries her. Once she gets close enough to the sofa, Charlotte lets go of Kim, who falls onto the cushions in a heap of gangly limbs, unconscious. Charlotte rolls Kim onto her back and heaves her legs onto the sofa for her, before sliding a small throw pillow underneath her head. Kim's mouth hangs open, a trail of drool leaking from the corner.

Charlotte can't help but feel another pang of regret at how she's been treating Kim. Although her jealousy is threatening to eat her alive and is making Kim's every action unbearable to her tonight, she knows that Kim has only ever genuinely loved her. She's always been there to provide feedback on every first draft, has attended every event, and has celebrated every one of her best friend's milestones.

Charlotte can't say the same about herself.

She brushes a strand of hair off of Kim's forehead, staring down at her face, before she turns to leave the room.

That's when she hears it.

The heaving. The gurgling. The coughs. Charlotte turns around.

Kim lies with her eyes closed on the sofa, only now her body heaves and struggles as she chokes on her own vomit. The contents of her stomach spill over her chin and spray onto her shirt as her body struggles to breathe. Kim should be getting up, should be rolling onto her side, should be doing something, *anything,* to stop herself from choking, but she's out cold and unresponsive.

Charlotte reaches for Kim, ready to turn the woman onto her side, ready to help clear her airway, ready to call 9-1-1, ready to—

I was really hoping we'd have books out at the same time again.

Charlotte freezes in her tracks, her hand inches away from Kim. She knows she should help her, but she doesn't.

Instead, Charlotte watches as Kim chokes and gags and heaves and sputters and, eventually, stops.

The house is silent.

In a haze, Charlotte stumbles to the entranceway and locks the front door before dragging herself upstairs. She crawls into bed fully dressed, lies on her side, and falls into an uneasy sleep.

———

IT'S NOT the light streaming through the open curtains that wakes Charlotte up but her pounding migraine. Pain shoots through her skull, lacing itself behind her eyeballs and burrowing deep into her temple. She checks the time on the alarm clock and exhales loudly; she has to wait another hour before she can take more acetaminophen. She grumbles to herself and rolls onto her stomach, burying her face in her pillow. She wants nothing more than to fall back asleep and forget about the drinking from the night before. Her tongue feels like cotton and the inside of her mouth tastes like the floor of a bar thanks to all the drinks she and Kim had last nig—

Kim.

Her chest tightens and she struggles for air as she slowly remembers her friend downstairs on the living room sofa. She pushes herself up in the bed, suddenly awake, and shakes her head.

No, there's no way, she tells herself, getting to her feet. She takes uneven steps across the bedroom floor, her body heavy from the alcohol and still slightly uncoordinated. She passes through the upstairs hallway and stops at the top of the staircase, holding onto the bannister with white knuckles.

"Kim?" she calls down. "Kim, are you up yet?"

The living room is silent.

"Kim?" she asks, louder. No answer.

She slowly descends the steps, using the extra time to convince herself that she's misremembering the night before as the downstairs comes into view.

She went home.

But she was drunk.

She took an Uber *home.*

Her purse is still hanging up in the entrance.

She's forgetful.

Her boots are there, too.

She's very forgetful.

Charlotte knows what she'll find waiting for her in the living room, so she goes into the kitchen instead and opens the blinds, the light making her migraine worse as she avoids looking at Kim's car in the driveway, buried under a thick layer of snow. She opens the pantry and takes out a bag of coffee, scoops some into her drip machine's reusable filter, and closes the lid before starting the appliance. She listens as the coffee percolates, enjoying the sizzle as condensation builds up and water drips onto the burner of the ancient machine. The smell of the dark roast is almost enough to cover up the smell of the spilt liquor and stale vomit.

With a slow exhale, Charlotte peers into the living room from the kitchen doorway.

Kim lies on her back in the middle of the sofa, her right arm spilling off the edge. Her mouth hangs open and streaks of liquid run down her skin, trailing onto the cushions underneath her head. Unlike last night, her eyes are now open and lifeless as they stare up at the white ceiling.

Charlotte stares at Kim for a long time before rushing to the bathroom, lifting the lid of the toilet in the nick of time, and throwing up. She heaves, the contents of her stomach from the night before splashing against the side of the white porcelain bowl and into the crystal-clear water. It burns the back of her throat as the alcohol and bile force their way out of her system. When she's finally done, she flushes twice before rising to brush her teeth and splash water on her face.

Trying not to look at Kim again, Charlotte goes back into the kitchen and grabs her phone off of the counter she had left it on last night. She unlocks the screen, glad to see there's still some battery left, and dials 9-1-1.

"9-1-1, what's your emergency?" the agent says on the other end.

Charlotte opens her mouth to answer but freezes, not sure what to tell them.

I killed my friend?

I let her drown?

I wanted her to die?

"Hello?" the operator asks.

"My friend," Charlotte finally manages. "I found my friend dead on my couch."

———

IT TAKES the ambulance twenty minutes to arrive at Charlotte's house while she waits on the phone with 9-1-1. She told them that her friend didn't have a pulse, wasn't breathing, and wasn't responsive, but they sent an ambulance anyway.

When the medics arrive to examine the body, they ask Charlotte the same questions the dispatcher had asked on the phone.

"How long ago did you find her?" one of them asks.

"About ten minutes ago. I came downstairs to put on coffee and I thought she was still sleeping. When I went to wake her up, I realized something was wrong."

"Where is she now?"

"Still on the sofa," Charlotte tells them, directing the pair to the living room, their boots trailing wet snow across the floor.

"Have you moved her?"

"No, I haven't touched her."

"Do you know if she's taken any medications or illicit substances?"

they ask her, transferring Kim from her spot on the couch to the wood floor.

"Alcohol."

"When?"

"We were celebrating for most of last night."

"Do you know how much she had to drink?"

"I don't know. A lot. We both had a lot. I wasn't feeling good, so I went upstairs to bed and left her alone. She was finishing a glass of wine on the couch when I last saw her," she lies.

The paramedics try to revive Kim but ultimately pronounce her dead. They tell Charlotte to leave the body alone until the coroner's office can come and collect it, then they give her their condolences and leave.

Charlotte pours herself a coffee and drinks it in the kitchen, focusing her attention on the sun outside the window. She doesn't want to think about Kim or her cold body lying in the middle of the room only a few short metres from her.

It's another two hours before the coroner's office arrives, their squeaky van parking at the top of her driveway. Two older men carry their gurney and a bag up the front steps of the house, and Charlotte leads them through to the living room. After examining the area and collecting Kim's body, they tell her that an autopsy will confirm Kim's cause of death but they suspect it to be aspiration pneumonia. They add that Charlotte is free to use her living room again and is allowed to clean or dispose of her sofa, as a police investigation into Kim's death is not necessary at this time. Like the paramedics, they offer Charlotte their condolences, before hauling Kim's body down the front steps. She watches from the kitchen window as they load the metal gurney weighed down with her friend into the back of the van and drive away from her home, the wheels of the vehicle spinning hard on the ice.

As she sits in the empty kitchen, the weight of everything finally hits her, and she cries into her hands. When she's done, she gets up and opens the fridge, pulling out the white pastry box Kim had brought her and taking out a cupcake with bright blue frosting and

edible pearls. She hums to herself, as she peels off the paper liner, the corner of her mouth lifting in a wry grin.

I guess our books aren't coming out at the same time after all.

FEBRUARY

"I'm so sorry for your loss," Emily says, leaning forward across the small table and taking Charlotte's hands in her own. "I know how close you and Kim were. I can't imagine any of this has been easy on you. Especially with the, well, you know," she says, gesturing to the room around them.

Charlotte nods tersely. She does know.

When her agent had called to meet with her off the clock for the first time since Kim's passing, Charlotte had been quick to suggest the bookstore by her house. Although it's just another Azure Pages, the largest book retailer in Canada with identical stores everywhere, the one near her house is outfitted with a coffee shop on the second floor. The drinks are never good and they cost her three times as much as it would to make them at home, but she's always loved coming here for the ambiance.

Unfortunately, Charlotte hadn't gotten the memo that all Azure Pages locations across the country were paying tribute to Kim's national legacy by plastering her name and face all over the store, along with endcap displays of her books. No matter where Charlotte goes in the store, it feels like Kim's eyes are on her.

She pulls her hands out of Emily's, who gives her a sad smile while she takes a sip of her coffee from the white disposable cup.

Those are so bad for the environment, Kim used to tell her, always making a point to bring her reusable mug wherever she went. *It's because of the plastic coating they use on the inside of the cups. You can't separate it from the paper, so it makes the cups impossible to recycle. You should really—*

"Yeah, I just can't believe she's gone," Charlotte says, drumming her fingers on the table.

"And it's been three weeks since she passed?"

"A month," she says, discreetly checking her phone for the time. "Wow, already?"

"Yeah, but it feels like it was only yesterday. The pain is so fresh, you know?"

As much as Charlotte hates to admit it, it *has* been a difficult couple of weeks for her. Since Kim's death, her house hasn't felt the same. There's a weight to the air inside the living room that wasn't there before her friend died, and the couch... she can't even look at the couch anymore.

To make matters worse, her phone has been blowing up with calls and messages from people looking to get more information about the circumstances of Kim's sudden death; everyone from reporters to friends to complete strangers has reached out to her. Although she was reluctant to say anything at first, worried that someone would somehow figure out what she'd really done—or, perhaps more accurately, hadn't done—to Kim, she soon realized that this was an opportunity she couldn't pass up to get her name out. While she's never so gauche as to promote her new novel outright, she doesn't hold back the details of its release whenever she's asked how she knew Kim.

"I can't even imagine what you must be feeling right now," Emily says now, eyes welling up out of sympathy for Charlotte. "I know we've mostly had a working relationship, but I mean it when I say I'm here for you if you need anything."

"Thanks, Em, I really, *really* appreciate it, but I think, right now, the best thing for me is to try and focus on other things, you know?"

"Oh, of course. But when you're ready, I'm here for you."

"Thanks," Charlotte says with a small, grateful smile.

Emily nods and leans back in her chair as Charlotte takes another deep sip of her drink. It's clear that the other woman wants to ask her something, but Charlotte is eager to leave the store and the watchful eyes of the cardboard Kims. She checks the time again as Emily bends down, searching for something in her large purse which rests on the floor next to her chair. She takes out a galley—the white sheets of a manuscript bound together but still coverless—and puts it face down on the table.

"Look, I told the publisher I didn't feel right asking you about this, but they were insistent," she says, shifting uncomfortably in her seat and avoiding Charlotte's gaze. She pushes the galley towards Charlotte but leaves her hand on the back of it when Charlotte reaches for it. "You're allowed to say no, okay?"

Charlotte picks the book up and flips it over, revealing the title page with a note written in pen.

OF CHAMPAGNE PROMISES
by Kim Lavoie

Note: Please keep the foreword to <500 words due to space constraints. Please return by March 1st for production deadline.

Release date: April 11th.

She stares at the ink on the clean white paper, her mouth bone dry and her chest tight. It feels like she's breathing air through a straw and her hands shake as she grabs the table to keep herself from falling over in her seat. She looks up from the page, eyes flickering around the interior of the book shop like she's searching for help. All she finds are the disapproving smiles of Kim, who watches her from the posters all around the store.

Charlotte tries to find the right wording but eventually settles on a simple, "What the fuck is this?"

"It's Kim's new book."

"I pieced that much together," Charlotte hisses. "But what do they want from me?"

"They want you to write the foreword for it, since you were Kim's best friend. She always talked about how close you both were, so naturally, you were the obvious choice for this."

"But her book isn't coming out. She's dead. They wouldn't put out her book this soon after she—"

"I thought it was in bad taste too, but the publisher wanted to move forward with it and her family has given them their blessing, so it's still coming out in April. Which is great because it means you'll get to share a new-release shelf with her one last time."

I was really hoping we'd have books out at the same time again.

Charlotte stares down at the manuscript, her face flushed and her lips dry.

"But if you're not up to it, I understand," Emily adds.

Charlotte looks up from the white pages and stops, her body freezing and heart skipping a beat.

Kim stares back at her from right behind Emily.

"What the fuck?" Charlotte shouts, standing up from her seat so quickly that her chair tips over and crashes onto the ground behind her, drawing her gaze. When she looks back up, Kim is gone.

Emily clutches her chest and leans away from Charlotte in her seat. "I'm sorry! I just... They asked and I thought you might be okay with it! I'll tell them no!"

Charlotte cranes her neck, trying to spot her dead friend in the sea of patrons. People are watching her with confusion, her sudden outburst having attracted the attention of both customers and staff. They eye her with worry, uncertain if she's about to have another outburst. When she doesn't see the Kim lookalike again in the crowd, she leans over the second storey bannister to stare at the customers in the bookstore below. If any of them heard her yell, they're not paying attention now as they browse the rows of books, reading back covers and putting novels away on the wrong shelves. The only Kims she sees now are on the posters, watching her with their manufactured smiles.

Charlotte exhales through pursed lips before she picks up her chair, drags it back to her spot at the table, and takes a seat across from her agent.

"Are... are you okay?" Emily asks, clutching the gold chain she wears around her neck.

"Sorry, I just..." She trails off, not sure how to finish her sentence. *Saw Kim? Saw something? Lost my mind?* She shakes her head apologetically, gesturing around the Azure Pages and at the manuscript. "I got really overwhelmed. It's been a lot, you know?"

Emily nods, on edge but warming back up to Charlotte. "I can't even imagine."

"I'm sorry I freaked out. That wasn't okay of me."

"No, you don't need to apologize for anything! I shouldn't have told them I'd ask you about the—"

"I'll do it. I'll write the foreword."

"Really? Are you sure?"

"Of course. There's nothing else I'd rather do to honour Kim's memory," she lies.

———

CHARLOTTE CLOSES the car door and locks it with the key fob before resting her head on her steering wheel, exhausted. Emily left almost fifteen minutes earlier, and Charlotte is thankful for the alone time without having to worry about whether her agent will stumble upon her like this in the driver's seat of her car. Especially when she's likely still freaked out by Charlotte's outburst in the coffee shop.

I was really hoping we'd have books out at the same time again.

"Fuck! Fuck! Fuuuuuck!" Charlotte screams at the top of her lungs, face buried in the leather steering wheel. She's furious with Kim, Kim's publisher, and—although she doesn't want to admit it—herself.

She can feel the question rooting around the back of her brain, weaselling its way into her train of thought.

Did I let Kim die for nothing?

She shoves her keys into the ignition, the engine roaring to life, and puts the car from 'park' to 'drive.' As she's pulling out of the Azure Pages parking lot, she swears she can still see one of Kim's posters watching her from inside the store.

———

SHE HANGS her keys on the hook by the door and kicks her boots off onto the plastic mat in the entranceway, reminding herself all the while that spring is nearly here, before unzipping her coat and hanging it in the small closet. She fishes Kim's galley out of her purse. The manuscript feels heavy in her hands despite its meagre size, and Charlotte wants nothing more than to throw it into her recycling bin and forget that she ever met with Emily at the Azure Pages.

Unfortunately, she knows that's not an option, and she brings the book into the kitchen with her and sets it down on the butcher's block.

OF CHAMPAGNE PROMISES
by Kim Lavoie

She rolls her eyes at the title. She's always thought Kim picked gaudy names for her books that would keep readers away, not that anyone—or even Kim's sales—agrees with her on the matter.

It's always frustrated Charlotte how successful Kim has been with her writing in comparison to herself. She's always thought that her own work is more meaningfully created, insightful into the human condition, while Kim's is, at times, tawdry and pedestrian. It bothers her that the masses don't agree.

Charlotte flips the book open, eyes glazing over as she scans the publisher information and legal jargon. She turns to the next page and stops at the dedication.

Charlotte,
I wouldn't be where I am today if it weren't for you.
Your friend, forever, Kim.

She exhales slowly, gripping the counter as she steadies herself, her eyes watering. The emotions hit her like they have these past four weeks: in waves of grief and regret that come unexpectedly and grab at her, threatening to pull her under, before letting her go just as quickly. As much as she's had moments throughout their long friendship where she disliked Kim—even wondering if she hated her at times—she still loved her, in her own confusing and conflicted way, and looked to her as a source of comfort. Although Charlotte had been guiltily glad to be rid of her in the moment, thinking Kim's absence could make room for her to finally get the recognition she deserves, she hadn't anticipated just how much she'd miss her friend.

She closes the book and wipes her tears with the back of her hand as the familiar sadness slowly releases its hold on her. She doesn't want to waste her evening crying over Kim, but she doesn't know if she'll be able to get through the book while sober. Charlotte opens the small cabinet above her kitchen sink, the hinges squeaking despite being fairly new. She takes out a wine glass, carelessly smudging fingerprints onto the crystal-clear bowl, before pulling open one of the stainless-steel doors of the fridge. She grabs a half-full bottle of white wine and pours herself a generous amount, enjoying the sweet floral bouquet, before returning the bottle to its shelf.

She leans against the island and takes a swig from her glass. She swallows fast, lips puckering from the harsh flavour that coats the inside of her mouth and drips down her throat.

"Ugh!"

The alcohol is bitter and overly acidic, like it's gone sour. She swirls the wine around in the glass, smelling it, nostrils flaring at its pungent scent. It didn't stink when she opened the bottle, but now it fills the air with a rancid odour. She makes a face and dumps the remainder of her glass down the kitchen sink before getting the bottle back out of the fridge to pour out the last of it.

The smell fills the kitchen and makes the air feel thick. Her head swims. She waves a hand in front of her nose, trying to disperse the smell, but it only makes her feel dizzier. She leans against the counter, noticing Kim's book out of the corner of her eye, and grabs the galley before escaping the stink of the kitchen for the fresh air of the living room.

She tries not to stare at the couch that Kim died on, but she can't help herself.

Charlotte avoided the living room for the first week after her friend's death. There was something about the room that made her uncomfortable, made her feel *guilty*, and so she started spending more time in her kitchen and up in her bedroom than she ever had before. Of course, having watched Kim die, it made sense to her at first that she'd have trouble being around where it happened. But then the feeling only got stronger, so much so that Charlotte couldn't help but be overcome with dread every time she set foot in the living room.

Not wanting to annex off a part of her house, she decided it wasn't the living room that was the problem but the couch itself. Although she'd had the fabric professionally cleaned, something about the sofa and its worn down cushions left her unsettled, so she bought a cover for them hoping it would help.

It didn't.

While the couch certainly looked different—the vintage plum cushions now covered with flamingo pink and decorated with throw pillows in gaudy floral covers reading things like "Home Is Where the Books Are!" and "Plans Were Meant to Be Cancelled!"—it still made Charlotte uncomfortable. The cushions where Kim had fallen asleep looked perpetually weighed down. No matter how much she fluffed them, no matter how much she rearranged the couch covers, and no matter how many blankets she piled under the cushions to lift them higher, they constantly looked flat.

Like Kim was still lying down on them.

A chill passes down Charlotte's spine and she looks away from the couch, moving through the room to her comfortable leather recliner stationed across from the sofa. She stumbles, her feet heavy as she moves, and she realizes that it's not the smell from the kitchen that's gotten to her but the wine itself.

She's drunk.

Her head feels fuzzy, her thoughts like the white noise and crackling static of a dead TV channel, and her every step is clumsy and fumbling. Her mouth is dry like sand and her face is hot to the touch. She falls onto her chair, dropping the galley onto the ground beside her. Her head lolls forward and she feels nauseous. With how uncoordinated she's become, she can't help but worry that she won't make it to the bathroom in time if she needs to hurl.

She blinks, confused as to how one sip of spoiled wine could send her over the edge, and she sees her.

Kim.

Lying on the couch.

Charlotte's heart beats so fast that she's sure it's going to give out at any second. She stares at her dead friend who looks up at the ceiling, unmoving, with a blank expression on her face, her mouth hanging open like it did the night she died. Her chest is still and she doesn't blink, but there's something about her that makes Charlotte feel like she could jump up at any second.

"K-Kim," she finally breathes.

Her friend is silent.

"Kim? I-sthatyo-ou?" she slurs.

Kim remains quiet, body still, and Charlotte opens her mouth to say something else but stops, sucking her breath in as Kim turns her head towards her. The other woman's eyes are hollow, empty, and they don't look *at* her, they look *through* her. Charlotte feels sick as Kim lies silently on the cushions with her gaze fixed on Charlotte's face. She can't look away as liquid begins to leak out of Kim's open mouth, colourless droplets spilling over her lips and running down her chin and over her cheeks, dribbling onto the light couch covers and leaving wet trails down the side of the sofa.

———

CHARLOTTE SITS up in her recliner with a start, her cellphone's ringer blaring in the entranceway. She stares at the sofa, her muscles tensing and pulse throbbing under her skin as she prepares herself to see Kim lying on the wet cushions, watching her.

But the couch is empty.

Her phone goes momentarily silent in the other room before ringing again, her cute ringer sounding obnoxious in the silence of her home. She gets up from her chair with a groan, her head pounding and stomach churning, and drags herself up to the entrance. She reaches into her purse, searching through her belongings for her phone, before pulling it out on the last ring.

"What?" she asks, not in the mood for pleasantries.

"Where are you?" Emily shouts, making Charlotte wince.

"I'm at home, why? What's wrong?"

"I've been calling you for like an hour! You were supposed to do that interview with—"

"Oh, shit!" Charlotte groans, slapping a palm to her forehead in frustration. The sudden jolt seems to jar her sore head and she squeezes her eyes shut in pain. "I completely forgot!"

"Yeah. They weren't exactly thrilled about being stood up."

"I'm sorry, I didn't mean to. I just, I don't know, I overslept."

"I figured as much. Thankfully, I was able to reschedule it with them."

"To when?"

"Check your email. I sent you a calendar invite."

"Thanks," Charlotte says, relieved.

"Try not to miss that one too, okay?"

"Sorry, Emily. Really, I am."

Her agent sighs on the other end of the line. "It's fine. I told them you've been having a hard time lately and needed the day off because of everything with Kim."

Charlotte can't help but laugh. "You're not wrong there."

"You know," Emily says, hesitantly, "you *really* don't have to write that foreword if it's too difficult right now. I know Kim's death hasn't been easy for you and—"

"It's fine. Really."

"I just mean that—"

"I need to go. Sorry, I'll talk to you soon. Thanks for rescheduling the interview."

She hangs up before Emily can say goodbye.

The hair on the back of her neck bristles and the air behind her feels heavy. She spins around, half-expecting Kim to be back in the living room, lying on the couch, judging her with dead eyes.

But no one's there.

She exhales loudly and rubs at her chest with one hand, feeling her heart beating fast beneath her breastbone. She lifts her phone again and types a few keywords into her browser, hitting search. She dials the first number that shows up on the screen.

"Hey there! I was just looking to book a mover. I have a couch that I need to get rid of."

———

CHARLOTTE THANKS THE BARISTA, slipping a fiver into the tip cup before heading to her favourite seat in the Azure Pages coffee shop. It's a small table hidden away from the perpetually long line of patrons and out of reach from the handful of power outlets people always seem to need to use. It's also, crucially, next to the shop's second-story bannister, allowing her to sip her coffee upstairs while looking out into the stacks of books below. Although it is one of the noisier seats in the cafe, allowing both the sounds from the Azure Pages and the coffee shop to crash over her, it's still her favourite spot to relax.

She places *Of Champagne Promises* on the round table and sips her expensive drink. As much as she hates carrying Kim's galley around in public, she hates the idea of reading it at home even more. The feeling in her house has only gotten worse since her dream about Kim on her sofa a few nights ago. Although she knows it's all in her head, likely a result of the stressful day she'd had with Emily, she can't shake the feeling that she's never alone in her house anymore.

The thought chills her and so she takes an even bigger sip of her drink to try and warm her bones back up.

OF CHAMPAGNE PROMISES
by Kim Lavoie

Charlotte opens the galley, making sure to skip past the dedication and the customary note from the publisher explaining that the book has been published posthumously at the request of Kim's family and with the blessings of her friends. *Which* friends gave the book their blessing, Charlotte will never know. She certainly didn't. Although she's agreed to write the foreword for the book, shamefully hoping that displaying her name in Kim's final novel might help her own sales, she has no intention of actually reading the manuscript.

As she flips through the pages, a sentence a few chapters in catches her eye. She takes a large sip as she reads:

'You must be excited,' Riley says, taking a seat at the mahogany table as Willow puts out a set of old champagne flutes that were gifted to her at her wedding.

'I am! But it's really not that big of a deal. I kind of feel silly celebrating, to be honest,' she says, blushing scarlet.

'Why would you be embarrassed?'

'I don't know. I just, I guess it's not that big of a deal,' she says, trying to downplay the importance of her situation.

Charlotte stares at the page, struggling to swallow as the hot drink burns her mouth. She reads ahead, not wanting to continue but unable to stop herself.

'It's a huge deal,' the woman argues. 'You have a book coming out! What's not to get excited about?'

'I don't know. I mean, it's not like it's my first one. And there are bigger names in the business...'

'So?' Riley cries. 'Don't seF yourself short! Oh, this is going to be so great! I was really hoping we'd have books out at the same time again!'

'Wait... are you saying that—'

'Yes! I wanted to wait to tell you in person because it's so exciting, but we have books coming out at the same time!'

'I'm so happy for you!' Willow shouts, disingenuous.

'Come on!' Riley lifts her champagne glass high in the air. 'To our success!'

Charlotte feels like the walls of the Azure Pages are closing in on her, slowly encroaching on her peace of mind and personal safety. She looks up from the galley and around the store, eyes immediately zeroing in on one of the large posters of Kim hanging from the ceiling.

It looks... wrong.

Kim's picture-perfect smile is gone, replaced by a blank expression and dull eyes. She stares down at Charlotte from her poster's spot high in the air. Charlotte looks away but finds herself locking eyes with another poster of Kim, this one looking up at her from its position on an endcap in the store below. Her pulse quickens as she looks around the room, spotting yet another poster of Kim near the entrance of the cafe. This one looks to the left, eyes seeing her through the doorway. She whips her head around, finding each poster of Kim and realizing the same thing over and over again: it's not a trick of the light, each photo *is* looking straight at her.

A hundred Kims, all watching her.

She slams the book closed, gets up from her spot at the table, and hurries to the escalator, breathing hard and fast.

All of the faces turn and move, their dead eyes following Charlotte as she leaves.

———

"I'M NOT TRYING to harangue you, Charlotte," Emily chastises over the phone, "but the deadline is in a couple of days and I haven't even gotten a draft from you."

"I know, I *know*. I'm working on it. You'll get it tomorrow."

"Will I? Actually? Because you've told me this twice now, and each time I check my inbox, I don't find anything from you."

"I mean it," Charlotte says, running a hand through her hair as she leans back in the bed, trying to get comfortable against the stack of pillows propped up between herself and the wooden headboard.

"Good, because I'm counting on you. You had me tell the publisher that you were going to write this foreword, despite my better judgement, and now they're pestering me to pester you."

"I know, I *knooooow*," she moans. Her laptop sits open on the comforter beside her, the black cursor blinking on the empty white page. "I'm almost done," she tells her agent, wondering how to even start.

"Tomorrow, Charlotte. I want to see it in my inbox. Got it?"

"Sir, yes sir," Charlotte jokes, saluting to herself.

"If it's not in by tomorrow morning, I'm telling them you're not going to write it."

"Fine," she grumbles. "Have a good night, Em."

"And you have a productive one," Emily says, the line going dead.

Charlotte clicks the power button on the side of the phone, her screen fading to black. She catches her reflection in the blackened glass, trying not to notice the bags under her eyes, her wiry hair, or Kim's eyes staring back at her from the screen.

She throws the phone onto the bed and slides the computer back onto her lap, pressing the backlight button a few times to make sure the screen is bright enough that it's blinding. She focuses on the cursor, avoiding the empty space on the monitor where she knows Kim's eyes now live.

Her friend's hollow stare followed her home from the store over a week ago and has infected her life ever since. Old photos of Charlotte and Kim no longer look like happy memories but are instead reminders of what she'd allowed to happen, reminders of what she'd done. Then she started seeing Kim's eyes in the empty spaces between, like when she's looking in the mirror or into the reflection of the TV or even at night in the blackness of her home. It's always the same: just two expressionless eyes watching her from somewhere that isn't *here*.

She clicks away at the keyboard, trying not to notice the eyes in the top right of her screen as she works, hoping they'll go away but knowing they won't. As she hammers out a poor excuse for a foreword, her computer flashes a warning: BATTERY AT 5%.

She reaches for the power cord, sliding her hand across the comforter as she searches for it before she remembers that she left it downstairs on the kitchen island. She exhales loudly. She doesn't want to have to go downstairs. Not with Kim just—

She tries not to finish the sentence in her mind, worried that she might give the idea power by even imagining her dead friend just—

She shakes her head, stopping herself again. She gets up from the bed and steps quickly through the second-floor hallway and down the stairs. She tries to avoid looking into the living room, afraid of what she'll see there, but she can't help herself as curiosity gets the best of her. Her new sofa sits where the old one used to, with a modern design and crisp marigold yellow fabric that pays homage to sofas of the seventies. It's not quite what she wanted, but she was desperate to get something, *anything*, to replace the sofa that Kim had died on, with its cheap cover and sunken cushions.

When the movers had come for the old couch, it had felt like a weight had been lifted from her life. Although she'd only seen Kim in her living room that one time, she'd avoided being around the sullied furniture since the apparition. It had taken nearly a week for the store to deliver her new sofa, and while the air in the house hadn't felt any lighter—even though Charlotte tried pretending like it had—she'd felt a bit safer.

But after the new couch had been delivered, she'd realized how wrong she'd been. Even before the movers had left, the cushions had started to look weighed down and sunken in, like someone was laying on them. She'd tried refusing the delivery but had already signed the papers. When she'd called the store with her complaints, they'd sent another team to collect the sofa and replace it with one that wasn't defective. But when the team came, no one but Charlotte could see the indents in the cushions. They still replaced the new couch with an even newer one, but the cushions were flat again when they left.

They're still flat now as Charlotte looks into the living room from the doorway of the kitchen. Although the couch unsettles her on its own, it's worse when Kim is there, lying on the sofa with her dead eyes looking up, always staring, like she can see through the floor and into Charlotte's bedroom. After the initial apparition that she'd written off as a dream, she didn't see Kim again for almost two weeks. When she did, it was while she was in the kitchen making toast. She felt something in the other room, like the air was heavy once more, and when she peered into the living room, Kim was back on the sofa staring into nothingness.

And then, in another blink, Kim was gone.

It happened again the day after, when Charlotte was in the entranceway pulling on her boots to go for a walk. The couch was empty and then, suddenly, it wasn't. She'd gone for her walk, hoping the crisp air would clear her head, but when she returned home, Kim was exactly where she'd left her. She stayed there for the better part of the day before vanishing into thin air and leaving Charlotte alone once again. Each time she appeared it was the same: she lay on her back in the middle of the couch, her arm spilling off the sofa and hanging onto the ground, dead eyes looking up at the ceiling. Each time she appeared, to Charlotte's frustration and mounting dread, she stayed a little longer.

Thankfully, the room is empty tonight and Charlotte breathes a sigh of relief as she grabs her power cord off the kitchen island. She turns around but then pauses, deciding to take advantage of the empty first floor while she has the chance. She quickly brews herself a tea and assembles a peanut butter and jelly sandwich before heading back upstairs.

As she leaves the kitchen, she sees Kim.

Although she's still in the living room, she's no longer on the couch. Instead, she stands at the head of the sofa where Charlotte stood the night Kim died, and stares at her friend with her dead eyes and her vacant expression.

Charlotte runs up the stairs, spilling the hot tea over the edge of the mug and onto her hand as she moves. Even after she slams the door behind her, she can feel Kim watching her from the living room below.

MARCH

Charlotte takes the keys out of her purse and slides them into the lock but doesn't turn them.

Not yet.

She leans her head against the cold wood of her front door and steadies herself, mentally preparing for whatever is waiting for her inside. Except she knows what's waiting in her house. It's the same thing that's been tormenting her for over a month now: Kim.

She sighs and turns the keys, the tumblers clicking into place as the door unlatches and swings slowly open. Her house is dark, the only light coming from the microwave that hangs over the range. The radio plays softly on the counter, some glam rock song from the eighties that she recognizes but can't sing along with, and she closes the door behind her. She hangs her jacket up along with her purse, kicks her shoes off onto the mat, and keeps her eyes glued to the floor—trying to ignore Kim's reflection in the hardwood—as she moves from the entrance into the kitchen.

She flips the switch on the wall, the room quickly filling with light, and she picks up the silver kettle off of the stove, ignoring Kim's reflection in the dull metal, before filling it with water. She sets it down on the burner before grabbing a mug, throwing in an Earl Grey tea bag, and adding two spoons of sugar into the empty ceramic cup. She leans against the counter, staring down at her feet, while the water boils. She doesn't need to see Kim's dead eyes in the kitchen tile to know she's being watched by the other woman.

Kim's movements around the house have been getting progressively worse. At first, she'd just lain on the couch, looking up at the ceiling. Then she'd started standing at the head of the sofa, watching Charlotte's every move. Then she'd started roaming the ground floor. Charlotte had discovered this while washing her hands in the bathroom, trying not to notice Kim's eyes in the hollows of the mirror. She'd opened the door to find Kim waiting on the other side of it. She'd screamed and locked herself in the washroom for almost thirty minutes, hyperventilating, before she'd finally found the courage to leave the room. The next time it had happened, Charlotte had been in bed sleeping when she'd felt Kim's presence in the room with her. When she'd opened her eyes, Kim had been standing at the foot of her bed, watching from the blackness. Charlotte hadn't gotten much sleep that night, or any of the ones that followed, for that matter.

Much like she's grown to accept Kim's eyes in the empty spaces of her life, or her dead body on the sunken living room cushions, she's eventually grown to accept that Kim will appear—and disappear—around the house at random. But just because she's come to accept the fact of it doesn't mean she can stand the feeling of those empty eyes staring back at her, and so she avoids looking anywhere she doesn't have to.

The kettle hisses and howls, filling the small space with noise. Charlotte turns the burner off, picks the kettle up by its heat-resistant handle, and pours the scalding liquid into her cup. She takes a metal spoon and stirs everything together in her glass before putting the utensil on the counter and leaving her tea to steep.

Her phone buzzes in her pocket and she fishes it out, making sure the screen is illuminated—the bright light helps drown out Kim's stares—before she looks at it. It's an advertisement forwarded by her agent. She scans the email.

I wasn't sure if you were on the mailing list for these notifications, but I

thought I'd pass them along in case you wanted to see them. If you don't, or if it's too much, just tell me. I'll make sure they don't come your way.
   — Emily

Charlotte scrolls down to the forwarded email, reading the header to herself.

An Excerpt From The Surefire Hit OF CHAMPAGNE PROMISES
Kim Lavoie's Final Novel, Available Everywhere April 11

The words strike a chord and she can't stop her eyes from watering as she rereads her friend's byline. It's Kim's last book, but in her heart she knows it didn't have to be. She just wanted her chance to make it big, to have her moment, to be recognized for her *art*, but even in death Kim overshadows her. The more she thinks about the night Kim died, the more she's filled with regret.

She keeps reading.

She laughs, letting go of the wooden chair and trying her luck standing on her own. Her legs shake and her body wobbles with each small step she takes as she tries to get to the leather sofa, her eyes struggling to stay open. Charlotte—

She rubs her eyes, sure she's reading the excerpt wrong, but the name is still there when she reads it a second time. Kim's eyes watch from the corner of her screen as she continues.

Charlotte is tempted to stick a leg out as Kim passes her by—

Charlotte thinks she's about to throw up.

—but stops herself when she imagines all the possible things the woman could crash into and break if she were to fall.

She skips ahead, stomach uneasy as she reads.

Kim's head lolls onto her chest and she struggles to walk, her feet dragging on the ground as Charlotte practically carries her. Once she gets close enough to the sofa, Charlotte lets go of Kim, who falls onto it in a heap of clumsy limbs and dead weight. She rolls Kim onto her back and arranges her on the couch, struggling to lift her legs onto the cushions and slide a small throw pillow underneath her head. Kim's mouth hangs open, a trail of drool leaking from the corner of the unconscious woman's mouth.

She shakes her head, unable to believe the words printed on the page.

She brushes a strand of hair off of Kim's forehead, staring down at her face, before she turns to leave the room.

That's when she hears it.

The heaving. The gurgling. The coughs. Charlotte turns around.

Kim lies with her eyes closed on the sofa, only now her body heaves and struggles as she chokes on her own vomit.

Charlotte holds onto the counter for support, suddenly lightheaded as she reads her own transgressions from that night, almost two full months ago, spelled out in the email.

Charlotte freezes in her tracks, her hand inches away from Kim. She knows she should help her, knows she should turn her onto her side, knows she should do something.

But she doesn't.

Instead, Charlotte watches as Kim chokes and gags and heaves and sputters and, eventually, stops.

The house is silent.

Charlotte drops her phone onto the ground, her hands sweaty and shaking as she tries to make sense of what she's read. She picks up the phone, face flushed and mouth dry, and skims over the email once more.

An Excerpt From The Surefire Hit OF CHAMPAGNE PROMISES

Kim Lavoie's Final Novel, Available Everywhere April 11

'No!' Riley screams, thrashing violently on the chaise longue.

But it's no use.

Strong hands hold her down in the dark and force her mouth open, chipping one of her teeth as the heavy glass bottle is forced into her mouth. The assailant covers her nose and forces her head back, the liquor burning its way down her throat as she coughs and chokes on it. She kicks out, trying to free herself as the bottle is removed from her lips, but soon another one takes its place and more liquid is poured down her throat.

Riley coughs, choking on the alcohol and getting dizzy fast. Everyone knows she's a lightweight and gets easily drunk off of a glass of wine. She doesn't want to think about what this will do to her.

She manages to land a kick in her attacker's gut, forcing them off of her and into the moonlight that streams through her curtains.

'You?' she asks, clutching her stomach and wobbling on her feet. It's the last thing she says before the world fades to black.

OF CHAMPAGNE PROMISES
The Final Novel of Kim Lavoie
Available for pre-order everywhere books are sold!

Charlotte stares at her phone for a long time before clicking the power button on the side of the device, shutting the screen off, too startled from what she's read to care that Kim's eyes watch her through the black glass.

Exhaustion hits her body like a brick, her legs turning to jelly and her eyes heavy. A migraine she didn't know she had pulsates behind her eye, and she decides to abandon her tea on the counter and go to bed. She turns off the kitchen lights and makes her way to the staircase, using the flashlight on the back of her phone to guide her.

Kim watches from the ground floor as Charlotte begins to ascend the stairs, her hand gripping the bannister tightly. She can't help herself and looks over her shoulder at Kim.

"I was really hoping we'd have books out at the same time again,"

Kim says as she looks up at Charlotte with her dead eyes and vacant expression.

Charlotte turns back to the stairs and heads to bed.

———

CHARLOTTE SITS in the living room recliner, her computer resting on her lap, and her eyes closed. She thinks of the sentence she wants to write, rewording it in her brain over and over again until it's perfect, before opening her eyes and typing it fast on the keyboard. She tries not to look at the eyes that follow her in the white screen of the laptop, tries not to focus on Kim watching her from the couch, and tries to tune out the blaring noise as she writes. Once the sentence is down, she closes her eyes and tries to focus on wording the next one.

Kim was always talkative in life and, much to Charlotte's ire, she'd grown talkative in death too. But where her voice was once light and melodic, it's now breathy and metallic, like she's whispering into a tin can. Even more frustrating to her is that Kim only repeats the same sentence.

"I was really hoping we'd have books out at the same time again."

At first, she'd said the line sporadically once or twice a day; then, she started saying it every hour. Now, she whispers to Charlotte constantly, a hum that doesn't stop and fills every corner of the house.

Having decided that any noise is better than the incessant whispers of Kim, Charlotte has been blasting the radio in her kitchen and keeps the television on 24/7. But even with the obnoxious commercials, eighties rock, and excitable talk show hosts, she can still hear Kim, a faint white noise that undercuts all the other sounds. She's so distracted by Kim's voice at the moment that she almost doesn't hear the doorbell.

She closes the laptop and rises from the chair, dropping the computer onto the seat behind her, staring at the floor as she moves through the house to answer her door. She keeps her eyes downcast and brushes a hand through her hair, knowing she's a mess. She hasn't been able to look in a mirror for a while, not without seeing Kim staring back at her. She turns the lock and opens the door.

Emily stands on her front steps, arms crossed over her chest and annoyance written on her face.

"So, you're not dead."

"What?" Charlotte asks, upset by the question.

"Well, I just figured you must be dead because you haven't been answering your calls or emails for the last week," Emily says, pushing past Charlotte and into the house. "Buuuut I guess you've just been ignoring me."

"Wait," Charlotte says, not turning around. She doesn't want to look back at Kim, who she knows is waiting for her inside her home. She wants to go out and have this conversation with Emily anywhere else. "How about we grab a coffee? My treat. We can talk about everything th—"

"I don't want coffee, Charlotte. I just want to know what's going on with you. You haven't been yourself since Kim died and I'm really worried about you."

Reluctantly, Charlotte closes the front door and turns to face Emily but keeps her eyes on the ground.

"I'm sorry. Things have just been really... stressful lately. I guess."

"Because of Kim?"

"Yeah," she admits.

"Have you thought about looking at therapy? Or maybe a grief counsellor?"

Charlotte shakes her head.

"Maybe it's something you should consider doin—Christ, why is everything so loud in here?" Emily interrupts herself, annoyed. She moves into the kitchen and turns off the radio before heading into the living room.

"Oh, no, please," Charlotte starts as Emily picks up the remote. "I like the noise. It's helpful and—"

Emily shuts off the TV and Charlotte finally looks up at her, trying not to let her distress show on her face. Kim stands directly behind Emily, her hushed whispers filling the space between them.

"How do you do anything with that racket? I could hardly hear myself think."

"I just... I prefer it." She doesn't add that anything is better than the sound of Kim's whispers. She doesn't imagine that would go over well with her agent.

"Look," Emily continues, her tone softening. "I need to know you're taking things seriously when it comes to the release of your next book. I think it's your best one yet and I want it to be successful. Don't you?"

Charlotte nods in agreement, although she struggles to hear Emily's words. Kim's whispers are loud and distracting, and she can't help but look around the room as she tries to avoid Kim's vacant eyes that watch her from behind the other woman.

"Good. Then I need you to put in the work. You can't keep cancelling interviews or public readings or any of the shit you've been doing," Emily says, frustrated. "I'm doing everything I can to help move preorders and get people excited about your novel before it comes out, but I can only do so much. *You* have to do the rest."

Charlotte nods again, eyes glued to Kim as Emily talks.

"I really need you to work at this," Emily says, a raspiness entering her voice. "You were so excited about this book, and now... it's like the love has died."

Charlotte looks back at the ground, the weight of Kim's stare too much right now.

"I'm sorry. I didn't mean to, I just—"

"I was really hoping we'd have books out at the same time again," Emily says, voice rattling.

Charlotte's eyes snap up, her heart jumping into her throat.

Emily stares at Charlotte with hollow eyes and a vacant expression. Her mouth hangs open and liquid pools over her lips and drips down her chin.

"What did you say?" Charlotte asks, voice small.

"I was really hoping we'd have books out at the same time again," she repeats.

"Kim?" Charlotte asks Emily tentatively. "Is that you?"

"Why did you do it?" Kim asks through the other woman.

"What?"

"I thought we were friends."

"We-we were."

"Were we?" she asks, moving towards Charlotte. Charlotte takes a step back. "You let me die. You didn't care and you let me die."

"Kim, I never meant to—"

"How could you just let me die?" She takes another step forward.

"I didn't mean to!" Charlotte cries, shoving Emily away from her.

Her agent falls backwards in the living room, crashing onto the floor hard. She looks up at Charlotte, her blank expression replaced by one of fear and confusion. Charlotte blinks down at her.

"Emily?"

"What the fuck is wrong with you?" Emily shouts defensively, pushing herself back up. Charlotte reaches out a shaking hand.

"I'm... so sorry. I thought—"

"Don't touch me!" Emily yells, yanking herself away from Charlotte and giving her a wide berth as she storms out of the room.

"Emily, I'm sorry! I don't know what happened. I just... Please, I'm sorry!"

Emily doesn't look back as she takes off out the front door.

————

CHARLOTTE'S PHONE vibrates on the coffee table as the email notification comes in. She looks down at the screen, unlocking the phone, and opens the email she's been expecting all week.

Emily has dropped her as a client.

————

CHARLOTTE SITS on the steps of her house, the clouds overhead threatening to bring rain. She doesn't care that it's cold or grey out. She's just relieved to be out of the house, even if she can still feel Kim's eyes on the back of her neck and hear the perpetual whispering.

She can hear it no matter where she goes.

She discovered this when she left her house to get groceries and Kim's whispers followed her all the way to the supermarket. She could see Kim's eyes in her back mirror and in the reflection of the store windows. She could see Kim in her backseat, in the parking lot, and at the end of every aisle.

It doesn't matter where she runs to, Kim follows.

But at least outside, she can find solace in the cold breeze and fresh air.

She watches her breath come out in white clouds, cutting through the air before fading to nothing. The day is still winter cold despite the lack of snow on the ground and she's excited for spring.

As she's lost in thought, a brown van pulls up and stops at the top of her driveway. A man gets out and opens the back, grabbing a small box out of the vehicle before approaching her.

"Char—"

"That's me," she says, not making eye contact. She already knows he'll have the same dead eyes and expressionless face as Kim. She holds out her hand and he passes over the small screen for her to sign. She scribbles her name and takes the box from him before he heads back to his van and pulls away.

With a sigh, she gets up from the steps and carries the box into her home, curious to know what's inside. She kicks her shoes off next to the door and passes Kim on the way to the kitchen. She grabs a knife from one of the drawers and runs it over the tape before throwing the utensil into the sink. She pulls back the brown cardboard and laughs when she sees the contents of the package.

OF CHAMPAGNE PROMISES
by Kim Lavoie

In addition to her advanced copy book is a small thank you note from the publisher raving about how much they loved her celebration of Kim's life and prolific career. She sets it down on the counter and flips open to the foreword she wrote and stares at the page in confusion.

I was really hoping we'd have books out at the same time again. I was really hoping we'd have books out at the same time again. I was really hoping we'd have books out at the same time again. I was really hoping we'd have books out at the same time again. I was really hoping we'd have books out at the same time again. I was really hoping we'd have books out at the same time again. I was really hoping we'd have books out at the same time again. I was really hoping we'd have books out at the same time again. I was really hoping we'd have books out at the same time again. I was really hoping we'd have books out at the same time again. I was really hoping we'd have books out at the same time again.

Feeling hysterical, Charlotte throws the book across the kitchen and hangs her head in her hands, trying to calm her breathing. Her eyes sting, her face feels hot, and all she wants is for Kim's whispering to stop.

But it doesn't stop. It never stops.

APRIL

Charlotte holds the book in her hands, running the tips of her fingers over the embossed cover, tracing her name on the thick paper. She should be happy, she should be filled with joy, but instead she feels... nothing. Not disappointment or sadness.

She just doesn't feel anything at all.

Kim stands across from her seat in the living room recliner, eyes wide and empty as she watches Charlotte, whispers filling the silence between them. The sound reminds her of rats in a wall scratching to get out.

She flips through the book, admiring the font and the stock of the paper. Even though her eyes scan each page, she doesn't bother trying to read anything. She knows it's pointless. The paragraphs all look the same to her now.

I was really hoping we'd have books out at the same time again. I was really hoping we'd have books out at the same time again. I was really hoping we'd have books out at the same time again. I was really hoping we'd have books out at the same time again. I was really hoping we'd have books out at the same time again...

She closes the book with a sigh, more exhausted than she's ever been in her life. She sees Kim's reflection in the glossy cover and feels the woman's eyes on her, Kim's whispering burrowing into her brain. Charlotte wants to scream, wants to cry, wants to do something, *anything,* to make the noise stop. She misses being alone in her house. It's been so long with Kim that she almost forgets what it's like not to be under constant observation.

"Happy release day, Kim," she says, looking up to stare at the other woman.

Kim looks blankly back at her.

"Let me guess," Charlotte continues, getting up from her chair and crossing the small room, "you were really hoping we'd have books out at the same time again?"

"I was really hoping we'd have books out at the same time again," she whispers.

"I thought you might feel that wa—"

"But you stole that from me."

Charlotte shivers, suddenly cold, and her heart beats faster. Although Kim has spent the last few weeks speaking at Charlotte, this is the first time she's ever spoken directly *to* her.

"What did you say?"

"You stole that from me. You stole that from *us.* Why did you hate me so much?" Kim continues, her face changing for the first time since her death. Sadness and confusion line her brow and the creases of her eyes, the corners of her mouth drawn downwards.

"I never hated you! I just—" Charlotte stops herself, throat tight. She can feel it again, the wave of grief that comes to pull her under when she least expects it.

"You just *what?*" Kim asks.

"I just wanted a chance to have what you did. I just wanted people to know my name."

Kim's expression hardens as she looks through Charlotte. "They will."

Kim advances on Charlotte, who backs away from her as quickly as her feet will carry her. Charlotte's throat begins to burn and her lungs ache as she tries to put distance between herself and Kim. She struggles to breathe, panic setting in, as Kim gets closer and closer. She coughs, trying to clear her throat. Clear liquid sputters over her lips and down her chin. It reeks of alcohol.

Kim takes another step forward and Charlotte tries to back away, but the backs of her knees hit the couch and she falls onto it.

"P-l-ease," Charlotte begs. "Puh-le-lease, Kim. I-I'm s-sor-ry."

Kim reaches out and puts a hand on her chest, pushing Charlotte down onto the couch until she's lying on her back. Charlotte kicks and flails, wanting to sit up, but she can't. The alcohol fills her mouth and burns a trail down her airway. She coughs as hard as she can, her body trying to fight as her lungs fill with liquid.

"I was really hoping we'd have books out at the same time again," Kim says with a sad smile, brushing a strand of hair off of Charlotte's forehead as she drowns.

The last thing Charlotte sees are Kim's dead eyes.

————

THE BOOK FEELS heavy in Emily's hand, and she thumbs through the pages with a heavy heart before putting it back on the display. She admires the design of the cover, the stylized art, and the sleek font of the title.

AND ALL THE RIVERS BURNED
by Charlotte Curran

A peach book-club sticker with a vibrant orange "O" at its centre has been fixed to each of the books. Emily can hardly believe the unexpected success that the novel has received since its publication, going so far as to make the New York Times Best Seller List in its first week of sales. She wants to believe it's because the novel is a work of art, a story that she and Charlotte believed in.

But she can't help but wonder if her former client's sudden and tragic death has helped bolster sales.

"I just... I can't help but wonder if I could have done something to help her, you know?" she says into her cellphone as she heads to the entrance of the Azure Pages.

Emily stops next to the exit, giving the store a final look before she leaves.

Charlotte stares back at her with bright eyes and a wide smile from the posters that hang from the ceiling and decorate the endcap displays.

With a sigh, Emily opens the door and heads out into the warm spring air.

DETAILED CONTENT WARNING

A Blackness Absolute: Detailed description of death via suffocation, enclosed spaces, tight spaces underground.

Sarah: Emotional abuse of a child, psychological abuse and neglect of a child, the mutilation of children, violence performed by a child.

The Broomway: Death via drowning, the death of a child. In Obeisance Park: Descriptive death of a child via magic, implied death of other children, graphic descriptions of decaying bodies.

Gordon: Medical paternalism, gaslighting, references to dementia, removal of bodily autonomy, elder abuse and neglect, death of an elderly woman downplayed to natural causes.

The Blue: Death via drowning.

Barmbrack: Death of a teenager via asthma attack.

Doireann: Death via starvation, the murder of a young adult, famine, illness, acts of cannibalism, references to death in a community.

Magnum Opus: Death via choking, alcoholism, abusive friendships.

ABOUT THE AUTHOR

Caitlin Marceau is a queer Canadian author and illustrator known for her award-winning novella *This Is Where We Talk Things Out*. Her forthcoming work includes her debut novel, *It Wasn't Supposed To Go Like This*, and her second novella, *I'm Having Regrets*. For more, find her on social media at @CaitlinMarceau or check out CaitlinMarceau.ca.

ALSO BY CAITLIN MARCEAU

This Is Where We Talk Things Out (2022)

All Roads Lead Us Home (2025)

Magnum Opus (2022)

Palimpsest (2022)

Femina (2022)

A Blackness Absolute (2023)

Loose Ends (2025)

It Bubbles Under The Skin (2025)

A Cold That Burns Like Fire (2022)